Praise for *Percival Everett by Virgil Russell*:

"Everett is one of the most gifted and versatile of contemporary writers. . . . His work takes hold of us and won't let go."   —Alan Cheuse, NPR.org

"Though funny, the novel also possesses a terrible and still sadness, concerning as it does not only William Styron and Nat Turner but also aging and death, the tragic hatred of racists, the depth of solitude at life's end. . . . The book, though it's frequently philosophical, is not in the least boring. Dear reader, how that impressed me! For there are times when philosophy can be less than action-packed. This is not one of them. Therefore, I heartily commend this book to you. . . . *Percival Everett* numbers among his very best."   —Lydia Millet, *Los Angeles Times*

"[A] stark, shattering novel. . . . The splintered stories keep their urgency even as they lose their drift. The note of sadness struck in the dedication swells and echoes through the wreckage of narrative, reaching a pitch of extraordinary anguish. This meta-fiction is deeply moving."
     —*The Wall Street Journal*

"A potent and thoughtful exploration of the bonds between fathers and children."   —*The Washington Post*

"Funny, insightful, and unpredictable. . . . Everett is a master of his trade."
     —*Time Out Chicago*

Praise for *Assumption*:

"Everett casts his line, as it were, pretty far, and some of the things he reels in, along with a few red herrings, are weighty indeed: racism, anomie, disillusionment, the meaning (or lack thereof) of one man's life—the American nightmare, in brief, at the end of the line. The setting, the protagonist and the eccentric and pathetic cast of characters will haunt you long after you close the book. I haven't read anything like it since Georges Simenon. And, as in Simenon's Inspector Maigret novels, the prevailing mood is one of existential despair."   —*The New York Times Book Review*

"[Percival Everett] is so original and ingenious that he defies categorization. . . . *[Assumption]* is a quick, bracing and ultimately enigmatic work about the deception of appearances—anything we take for granted, Mr. Everett means to show us, may turn out to be a lie."

—*The Wall Street Journal*

"[*Assumption* is] made up of three sections, with each one overturning its opening premise and taking us out into deeper waters. . . . All we can do is hang on and go along for the intellectually stimulating and genre-bending ride, in which bodies and assumptions fall quickly by the wayside."

—Alan Cheuse, "All Things Considered," NPR

"You think you know things about Ogden [Walker], and the killers he's pursuing, but Everett will chip away at every one of your assumptions until, in the very last pages, you're in an entirely different, much more unsettling story. Imagine sitting down with a Tony Hillerman novel and suddenly finding yourself in a Jim Thompson nightmare, but it's so compelling that you can't turn away. That's the ride Percival Everett takes readers on, and the one disappointment may be that there's absolutely no chance for a sequel."

—*USA Network*, "Character Approved"

"Well plotted and utterly unpredictable. . . . As always, this Everett novel is unsettling. Readers who prefer gift-wrapped endings should stay away. All other readers should enter."

—*Star Tribune* (Minneapolis)

Praise for *I Am Not Sidney Poitier*:

"A freewheeling coming-of-age of sorts . . . and one of the funniest, most original stories to be published in years. Everett has written a delicious comedy of miscommunication. From his narrator's unfortunate, hostility-inducing name to Ted Turner's constant non sequiturs, confusion reigns in this journey through the perception-warping, soul-twisting badlands of race and class."

—NPR, "Books We Like"

"One of the most talented contemporary novelists writing in English. . . . [Everett] is wildly inventive."

—*Star Tribune* (Minneapolis)

Glyph

Glyph

A Novel by
Percival Everett

Graywolf Press

This publication is made possible, in part, by the voters of Minnesota through a Minnesota State Arts Board Operating Support grant, thanks to a legislative appropriation from the arts and cultural heritage fund, and through grants from the National Endowment for the Arts and the Wells Fargo Foundation Minnesota. Significant support has also been provided by Target, the McKnight Foundation, Amazon.com, and other generous contributions from foundations, corporations, and individuals. To these organizations and individuals we offer our heartfelt thanks.

Published by Graywolf Press
212 Third Avenue North, Suite 485
Minneapolis, Minnesota 55401

www.graywolfpress.org

Published in the United States of America

ISBN 978-1-55597-667-5

2 4 6 8 10 9 7 5 3

Library of Congress Control Number: 2013946923

Cover design: Kapo Ng

For my dear friend and editor, Fiona McCrae

Deconstruction Pa~~per~~

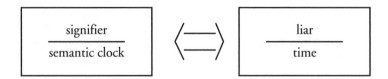

$$\frac{\text{signifier}}{\text{semantic clock}} \Longleftrightarrow \frac{\text{liar}}{\text{time}}$$

RALPH

A

différance

I will begin with infinity. It was and is the closest thing to me. I am a child and all I see is infinitely beyond my grasp, my understanding, my consciousness. But my unconsiousness is what my father and mother were just sick with anxiety over. They paced and worried aloud to each other about what I might sense in their tone, in their manner, but failed at every turn to attend to the very words they spoke, saying anything they pleased in front of me, wondering aloud to each other whether I had Uncle Toby's ears—*they're just so huge*—, commenting on my slow rate of attaining a full pate of hair, and above all else, paining at my seeming inability to adopt language. But while they stewed, I watched and contemplated potential and actual infinities and interestingly I found that there is no space between the two, that the arrow may indeed halve the distance to its target until the cows come home,[1] but the target and the arrow situated together in my field of vision were therefore in the same place and so the arrow was there and not there, making Zeno both right and wrong. My parents, however, clawing at speech like sick cats, could not fathom my lack of interest in parroting their sounds. They put their smelly mouths in front of my face, somehow assuming that without an ability to express offense, it could not be experienced, and formed words slowly, carefully, allowing me to

---

1. The cows, of course, remaining forever in the pasture, their bags fat with the milk Zeno awaits, are no more than the arrows, by extension. And finally, the infinite of the imagination, standing in necessary relation, because of its contrast to the infinite of self-relation, must be part of the signification of that thing from which it is separated by infinity.

observe where the tongue is placed for t's and how the lips peel apart for b's. They pointed to the table and said the name of that thing, assuming that I would learn not only to say it, but to recognize it. However, I did not see *table.* I saw where the plates were, what occupied the space beside my high chair. Bless their hearts, they were trying to teach me, to show me *tableness,* though I am lost as to why they did not simply say that.[2] But they were what they were, sadly, and that was speakers and for them infinity only moved in one direction and so it was only faith that had them believe that it actually existed. They peered ahead at the horizon and decided that the limit of their vision was merely the limit of their vision, accepting that the edge moved away with each step toward the horizon, assuming that their inability to define or delimit the limit itself did not negate the actuality of that limit. And so they kept looking at something that was not there, but that was also there forever, a kind of double gesture, *la double séance,* if you will, and they called it beautiful. If not insane, then they were at least dangerous.[3]

pharmakon

1

My father was a poststructuralist and my mother hated his guts. They did not know—how could they have known?—that by the age of ten months I not only comprehended all that they were saying but that I was as well marking time with a running commentary on the value and sense of their babbling. I lay helplessly on my back and stared up at their working mouth parts, like the mandibles of grasshoppers at work, mindless in their activity.

2

One evening, my father looked down at me, my mother standing beside him. He was not a fat man, but he was bloated, moving as if he were larger than he actually was. His face looked pulpy and I wanted to, and often did, squeeze his fleshy cheeks and pull. He hated that, and my insistence on

---

2. For it was certainly not the case that, when they pointed to themselves and made their vain and insipid pleas for utterances of *Ma-ma* and *Da-da,* they were trying to get me to recognize other parents in the world. So, why didn't they point and say, "Our breakfast table," or "the table that Uncle Toby gave us?"

3. Aside from the fact that they would throw me into the air and catch me like a ball, they, for all their stock in the words they babbled, often made meaningless sounds, which were not even good music.

doing it, coupled with my lack of speech, led him to say, "Maybe he's mildly retarded."

"Maybe, he's just stupid," my mother said and so stationed herself in my thinking as the brighter of the two. I smiled my baby smile at her, unnerving her on a level that her speech[4] kept her from knowing. "Look at him," she said. "He's smiling like he knows something."

"Gas," my father said. "He can't be stupid." He was bothered by the thought. "Look at me. Look at us. How can he be stupid?" What an imbecile.

"Lots of geniuses come from people of average or even less-than-average intelligence," she said.

Never were truer words spoken and they hung in the air like a tenacious perfume. My father fanned his nose and stroked the thin beard of which he was so proud and for which he cared like a garden. I looked away from his pudgy cheeks to my mother's soft features. Oedipal concerns aside,[5] I preferred the company of my mother, not simply because of the comfort of her softness and somewhat more compassionate nature, but because she possessed a native intelligence, a subhuman mind, though nothing negative is meant by that, an ability to abandon cohesion to what my father would call the signified. But he, for all his gum-bumping could not begin to understand not only the disconnection, but the connection itself, falling repeatedly into the same trap, the thought that he not only could talk about meaning, but that he could make it.

unties of simulacrum

Although they were well on their way to separate ways,[6] I moved things along one evening. I lifted my father's fountain pen from his shirt pocket as he was putting me down for the night. I was nearly one year old at the time and I used his pen to write the following on my crib sheet (pardon my pun):

---

4. And I do mean speech here and not language. Language was no more the villain than she and no less she than herself, as with me, as with you, but she spoke it with her lips and so, built a fence, a gap, which like the Stygian can be crossed but once.

5. Or not, as I find no shame in wanting *Inflato,* as I called him, if not completely out of the picture, at least shoved to one side or the other.

6. To different infinities, if you will allow, one infinity being no different from the next and so the same, but being necessarily different by simple reference.

why should ralph speak   ralph does not like
the sound of it   ralph watches the mouths
of others form words and it looks uncomfortable
lips look ugly to ralph when they are
moving   ralph needs books in his crib   ralph
does not wish to rely on the moving lips for
knowledge   ralph does not like peas
ralph is sorry he stole da-da's pen

The following morning I awoke to my mother screaming. "Douglas! Douglas!" she called to my father.

Inflato came running to her, his mouth frothy with teeth cleaner.

"Look," she said. "Look at that." She pointed into my crib. I scooted over so they could see better.

"It's not funny," Inflato said.

"I know it's not funny." She looked at him looking at her. "I didn't write it."

"Enough already. It's not funny."

"Did you write it?" she asked.

"No, I did not. Does that look like my handwriting?"

"Well, does it look like mine?" she shot back.

He stormed out. I could hear him spitting into the sink in the other room. My mother remained and she was staring at me. She believed that my father had not written the message and she knew that she had not and, barring some very strange intruder from this realm or another, I was the only other suspect. She left the room and returned quickly with a book, which she opened and handed to me upside down. I turned it over and began to read. She took it back and again gave it to me with the words turned over. Again, I righted the book and read.

"You understand?" she asked.

I nodded.

A weird giggle escaped from her throat and she swallowed it as quickly as it had been issued. She looked as if she were contemplating calling my father back into the room, but she didn't. "And you can read?" she asked.

I nodded once more.

She took the book and read aloud from the first page. At least, she pretended to read from it, as she made up some drivel about bears and a blond girl. I shook my head. She then read, "'One: The world is all that is the case. One-point-one: The world is the totality of facts, not of things.'"[7]

supplement

1

And so my mother became my supplier. She gave me magazines and novels and philosophy books and history texts and volumes of poetry. I consumed them all, trying to at once escape myself and stay as close to my own thought as possible, feeling more pure and freer with each turned page. Nothing in my mind became untied from the world, though I did experience a kind of self-erasure, a becoming transparent, and so allowed the words[8] to present themselves as what they were, referring to nothing other than their being. I was a baby fat with words, but I made no sound.

2

Books and nipples. Nipples and books. My lips were good at closing about that sweet red circle. The food had long ceased to be interesting, though it was far better than peas, and so the sucking, though routine (and not), is exercise in being. To say that it was like a raspberry is both inadequate and inaccurate, as I had no experience with anything but raspberry flavor. The breast itself was nothing, the nipple was everything. Once I spied my parents engaging in sex,[9] and I saw Inflato sucking away at my favorite nipple. I was not jealous, did not consider that he should not be there, but he was doing it all wrong. I was fascinated by the texture of it, like a relief map of another planet, perforated as it was by numerous orifices, apertures of the lactiferous ducts. He, with his clumsy tongue, was not treating it badly,

---

7. You, no doubt, recognize the text and of course, as the author would later point out himself, it was complete nonsense. But what nonsense. He loved the words, the pregnancy of them, how they swelled with meaning and at once fell stillborn from the page. I mention this to underscore that the reading was in no way speaking. Reading, amplified, is no crime, though it is unnecessary, not a luxury, just something that is not bad.

8. Ideas, words, concepts, puppies—all the same things. The world, things, signifiers, signified, pigs, planets, philosophers.

9. I do not say "made love." They no more made love than they made sex or made me. If I drop a hammer, it falls to the floor. I may drop it to the floor, but I do not make it drop to the floor.

but neither was he serving it justly. When they caught me staring, they stopped and began to laugh.

bedeuten

Boredom is the baby's friend. I would giggle when Inflato decided to toss me about like a sack of flour only to see if I might trigger some kind of gag reflex and so *spit up* on him. Boredom is not blind to anything, and certainly not to amazement. It is nothing close to amazement and I am not suggesting that somehow the meaning of one circles around to find itself almost that thing of which it is believed to be the opposite. Boredom is a high hill, a crow's nest, a hunter's blind (to use the word *blind* yet again), from which everything can be seen. And what better place to stand in observation of one's self, to be free of sensation and confusion.[10] *Taedet me ergo sum.*

spacing

Inflato yaks about the ongoing critique of reason, feels he is a part of it. I suppose he is as much a part as anyone else.

About rationality and Leibniz and Aristotle's conception of a principle of reason: Grog was being chased by a snake and so he leaped from one side of the stream to the other. Trog was waiting on the other side and said, "How did you ever get away from that snake?"

"I leaped," said Grog.

"Oh, that is leaping," said Trog. And though he had cleared the stream many times before in a similar manner, from then on he leaped. What was more, he could tell someone he was going to leap and tell them afterward that he had leapt.

Inflato took me to his office. I rode in a carrier on his back and observed, during our walk through the parking lot, the thinning of his hair. He kept talking to me and asking if I was "all right back there" and calling me "buster" and "little feller." We met a woman at the mailboxes and the back of his head took on a different spirit. He used me shamelessly, talked

---

10. Because, what is the confusion in boredom? It is simply what it is and can be nothing else, is safe for this fact. This is why people listen to rock 'n' roll and rap. It is the same. It is boring. It is finally an affirmation of everything, but an admission of nothing.

to me sweetly, but did not mention, mind you, that I was either mildly retarded or flat-out stupid.

The woman, who was younger than my mother, and perhaps prettier, but far less interesting, stepped around to look at my face and touch my nose. She cooed at me and I glared back. "He's so cute," she said. "How old is he?"

"Ralph will be one year old next month. Right, Ralph?"

"I can't believe the semester's half over already," the woman said.

"Would you like to have coffee sometime?"

ennuyeux

Amen. Fiat, fiat. Amen. My mother hated talking to my father, but she tried all the time. I could not tell whether he hated talking to her, but he seemed to avoid it, until it started and then he couldn't be silenced. Of course, my mother, knowingly or not, though I took her to be genuinely concerned, often approached Inflato badly.

"Whatever happened to that novel you were working on?" she asked.

He stopped eating, put down his fork, and said, "Fuck novels. I've found a better way of expressing myself. Besides, nobody is fooled by fiction or poetry anymore. Writing is the only thing.[11] Criticism is my art."

"What about after you get tenure?"

"I realize that all of this must be hard for you as an artist, the challenging of your station as superb creator, but what we're discovering about language doesn't diminish your worth, only that of your art."

My mother sat there, staring at him. If she could have, she would have struck him dead with a bolt of lightning. "You used to dream of being a novelist."

"That was childish," Inflato said. "I was a kid and didn't know any better. I used to think that novels were high art and mysterious, but they're not. They are what they are."

"You're rationalizing. You're a failed writer and you can't stand it." My mother drank some water and smiled at me. "Your son's going to be a writer."

---

11. I traced his source on this matter. "Poetry, novels, short stories are remarkable antiquities which no longer fool anyone, or hardly anyone. Poems, narratives—what's the use of them? There is nothing but writing left." J. Le Clézio, Foreword to *La Fièvre,* Paris, Gallimard, 1965. But I do not know how novels were meant to fool anyone. What are novelists and poets trying to do?

"He's cut out to be one, that's for sure."

"What kind of crack is that?"

I knew what kind of crack that was as well as she. The laughable truth, of course, was that Inflato was being so conspicuously seduced, or fooled, by the language he had chosen, though claiming a simple awareness of discourse. Had he truly been aware of what he was about with language then he would have shut up long before that and perhaps retreated to the reciting of Walt Kelly's or Lewis Carroll's nonsensical doggerels in his quest to make[12] meaning. He chewed with his mouth open and talked with his mouth full. *Rabbits are rounder than bandicoot's sam.* For Inflato, the subject of his failure as a writer forced a kind of reappraisal of agony and he didn't suffer with dignity, but like the coward he was, advanced with a pointing finger.

> *Aliquid stat pro aliquo*
> *Alterity*
> *Aufhebung*
> *Atopos*
> *A*

"So, you don't think what I do has any value," my mother said.

"I didn't say that."

"Then what did you say?"

"I can't believe we're finally rid of Nixon."

"Don't change the subject."

"Come on, Eve," said Inflato. "Your paintings can only be exactly what you are, a product of your culture."

"And your work?"

"I readily admit the same is true for me."

"But yet you put your name on your few articles and your perpetually near-completed book."

Zing! Zeno could have had no quarrel with that arrow.

"Fuck you," Inflato said.

"Fuck you, too!"

---

12. Or perhaps I should use the word *construct,* though it leaves a bad taste in my mouth, so to speak.

libidinal economy

And so for Inflato, from there on down it was uphill all the way.

peccatum originale

My mother, let me from here on call her Mo, put paint on canvases with a kind of abandon. Not a lot of paint, but with a wild hand I envied. There was great tension in her strokes, as if something, I am pressed to say what, was about to be catapulted somewhere. I was moved by the shapes and colors and whereas I recognized forms, trees, horses, houses, whatever, it was not to them that I attended, but something beyond them, or within them, or around them. And strangely her big paintings were as good as her small ones. But for all the colors and light she flashed on the surface, there was a blackness in her, a darkness of spirit[13] that I found not only compelling, but necessary. That part of her wanted to eradicate all form from her work (she loved Mondrian), but the conflict was too great, she saw too much, and was not so much unable to free herself from that vision as she was committed to killing it. And of course one cannot slay an absent dragon. *Kant was a cunning Christian.*

Mo was brushing gesso onto a large canvas when a man walked into her studio. I was in my monkey swing, a contraption that allowed me to stand and bounce, but finally was simply a way of chaining me up so that I could not waddle away or into trouble.

"Hello, Clyde," she said.

"Eve."

"I thought I'd take you up on your invitation." He turned a circle in the room, looking at the canvases. "Oh, my goodness," he said. "These are striking." He did not say they were good. I liked that. Mo liked that. "And this is the most beautiful creation here." He indicated me with a glance and

---

13. Nothing could be better or more attractive than a darkness of spirit. For I do not mean *evil*. And I do not mean dim light. It was as if she were born in some far-off land, lost from the world around her, it failing to accept her more than she failing to grasp it. Consequently, she craved some kind of attention, perhaps affection, not on a broad scale, but in a rather specific way that it was all too clear my father neither recognized nor understood. She was trying to save her own soul through her art and, bless her heart, she was trying to take me with her. She cried while she painted, wailed. But she could not, for all of her talent, take care of herself. A sad truth that it was clear to me she appreciated and so, sadly, was her reason for being with my father.

made my mother smile. The line was frankly a bit sickening, but it rang as genuine, so I let it pass and continued bouncing. "What's his name?"

"Ralph."

"Great ears," Clyde said.

Clyde turned back to the work. He walked to the far wall to look at a huge mostly ochre canvas. "I love this one," he said. "It's lonely though. I can feel you in it, but no one else."

I stopped bouncing and listened to Clyde.

"I see movement in a world that is frozen, but that's not to say that it feels cold. Does that sound stupid?"

Yes.

"No," Mo said. "That's exactly how I felt when I made it."

I knew this was true, and I was impressed by his acumen, but still to say such a thing. But, for me, to say anything was a bad beginning.

Mo and Clyde talked about painting for a while, until they were awkwardly silent and Clyde said that he had to go home.

ens realissimum

1

In this culture predispositions of the conquered and oppressed seep into the foreground; it is those of lesser intelligence who seek salvation or, at least, refuge in it. This is why, more often than not, they are Christians. I am subjugated in the same way—I'm a baby, for crying out loud—but I do not fall for it. I don't believe in sin. My body is not bad. I was playing with my willy just this morning. Inflato was shocked to find me touching myself and told me in a nice, but strained, tone not to do it anymore. He no doubt believed that my propensity for self-stimulation was connected in some way to my lack of speech and finally because of some holandric gene[14] the presence of which was his fault. The first thing the Christians did after they chased out the Moors was close the public baths.

2

Inflato hates his senses. He thinks they want to trick him.

---

14. See "New Data on the Problem of Y-Linkage of Hairy Pinnae," Stern, Centerwall, and Starker, *American Journal of Human Genetics,* 16: 455–71, 1964.

causa sui

1. Inflato kisses my mother stiffly, his lips hard, dry, unyielding like bricks and they have sex because they are married, because they must turn to each other for it. They own each other in that sense. They are each other's cars. Sex is maintenance. Mo is hurt by each routine spin around the block. She cries and the darkness in her swells ever greater and so, oddly, she is fed by it, the sickness, fed by the thing that kills her. But isn't that the human way? Kill the lamb for meat. Kill yourself for truth.

2. Inflato's scalp was dry, I noticed. It was a paricularly cold day and I was bundled up and wearing an itchy cap. There was a spring in his gait that day. We collected his mail, another rejection of his manuscript—this one from the University of Massachusetts Press—a nice enough letter. The bounce in his step persisted however as we left the building and walked a block to a nearby restaurant where we met the young woman.

3. Laura was not as pretty as my mother on second viewing. Her hair was well cared for and her nails were neat, but her eyes were clear in that bad way. From my perch on my father's side of the booth I could see into her eyes and I could see forever. I could see the horizon. Nothing stood between me and infinity. But even I, at my age, could see that whereas nothing stood between me and the back of her head, that same nothing stood between my father and her nipples.

4. Laura asked about my mother. Inflato told her that Mo was a artist and "a fine one, but she has bouts with insecurity."
   "That's too bad," Laura said.
   "It's really quite tiring. I find myself trying to build her up all the time. I mean, I want her to do well, but I've got my own work to do."
   "I read your paper on alterity," Laura said.
   Zing!

5. My father tried to give me a sip of his juice, then laughed with Laura at the face I made. She said I was adorable. He said I looked like my mother. Bastard. She asked him if they could get together another time. He say that he would like that. Then he put the itchy cap back on my head.

supernumber

The shadowy figure relaxing in the corner is four years old now, and tucked away writing this. Writing myself into being? I think not. Doing more than surface, novelistic rendering? I think not. All too aware, am I, of my large ears and frightening silence, a silence so intimidating that my parents run from me. My emotional makeup is a sculpture, a marble real-world representation of the real world. Buoys float in my tears and toy boats collect about the buoys. Mondrian considered his work "New Realism," claiming to see in nature what it was he represented, however cold and mathematical and even empty. Poor, poor Piet. But if that's what he saw. . . . The world I see has no hard edges like his and it is full of symbols, but not simply my symbols or my language's symbols, but reality's own symbols. We do not give the creature *reality* enough credit, choosing to see it sitting out there as either a *construct* of ours or an infinitely regressing cause for the trickery of our senses. But I claim here that the most important thing I have learned in my four years is that reality has a soul, reality is conscious of itself and of us, and further is not impressed by us or our attempts to see it. In fact, we see it all the time and don't know it, perhaps can't. It is like love in that way.

seme

Mo knew the essential thing. She knew that what she loved loved her back. It was not me, but the colors, the shapes, the stretcher bars of her canvases. They loved her and she could feel it. She never spoke of it and wouldn't. She wouldn't have understood the idea of speaking of it and as soon as she considered speaking of it, it would have become unintelligible. Mo was in that world too real to speak.

ephexis

"So, you had lunch today?" Mo asked.

Inflato picked me up to greet me in the living room and ignored the question.

"Well?"

"Did you have lunch with someone?"

"Yes. A graduate student. A woman who is interested in alterity."

incision

My mother fed me more and more books. I read the Bible, the Koran, all of Swift, all of Sterne, *Invisible Man,* Baldwin, Joyce, Balzac, Auden, Roethke. I read about game theory and evolution, about genetics and fluid dynamics. I read about Jesse James, Bonnie and Clyde, Joseph McCarthy. I read the service manual for my parents' '63 Saab, for the Maytag washing machine, for the Kenmore air conditioner. I came to know about the interactions of adults and the workings of machines, history, and the problems of epistemology. Experience was something I understood would be gained, but my comprehension of those things that had yet happened to me was substantial and solid. I dreamed about fishing with Hemingway and walking the streets of Paris with James Baldwin. I didn't know what flan tasted like, but I knew how one was made. I could picture the recoil of a fired shotgun and the damage done to the unsuspecting mallard. Through reading, I had built a world, a complete world, my world, and in it, I could live, not helplessly as I did in the world of my parents. I took the fuel dear Mo provided, but I did not use it immediately to write *Ralph on Ralph,* but to write poems. I wrote them on the pages of a loose-leaf notebook with a crayon (pen and pencils are dangerous) supplied by my mother.

> *The Hyoid Bone*
>
> *Brace the words,*
> *the delicate instrument,*
> *the tongue for sweet kissing,*
> *upsilon.*
>
> *Arch of bone,*
> *greater cornu, reaching,*
> *reaching, stretching*
> *above the lesser.*
>
> *Fracture this bone,*
> *by the violence,*
> *feel the sick*
> *pain of swallowing.*

Fracture this bone,
compromise the support,
feel the true anguish
of speech.

This was the first and it caused Mo to faint dead away. When she came to I was still in my crib staring at her.

"You wrote this?"

I nodded.

bridge

My father did not believe my mother when she presented him with my first poem. He didn't laugh, but looked at it and asked, "Okay, what am I supposed to say?"

"Your son wrote this," Mo said.

"Eve," he complained. Inflato looked over at me. I was standing in my playpen, holding myself up by the padded rail.

"He did," Mo insisted. She got up from the sofa and walked over to me with my notebook and a crayon. "Ralph," she said, "write something else."

I understood why she was asking and I sympathized with her situation, but I could not simply write on demand. I stared at the book, admiring the infinity of the blank page. Inflato made some kind of disparaging remark that might have been meant for Mo, me, or both of us.

"Oh, Ralph," Mo said.

I tried to shrug my baby shoulders.

"I'm going to the office," Inflato said. "I've got some papers to grade." He stopped at my pen on his way to the door. "Say 'bye-bye,'" he said.

I blew a raspberry through my lips.

Vexierbild

periscope depth

Inflato was beside himself with excitement. Roland Barthes was coming to visit the campus. Barthes was his hero and though Mo had slipped me a couple of books written by the man, I did not share my father's enthusiasm. I had read his *Elements of Semiology* and *S/Z*[15] and so he was no mystery to me. But Inflato was bouncing off the walls, singing and saying to my mother at the breakfast table that perhaps Roland Barthes would read his manuscript and then everything would be on track.

Inflato brought the great man home.

MO: Would you like something to drink before dinner?

BARTHES: To drink. Sometimes I drink. Sometimes I am consumed. Often I have an urge to commit suicide. But to drink on an overcast evening such as this. Tonight I will be engulfed.

Hinckley

INFLATO: Oh, my.

MO: So, wine then.

BARTHES: To start from a dream: If I slip, fall, and hurt myself in a dream, where is the cause of my fall? If it is a banana peel on which I slip, then is it in my dream or is it in the real world, where there are banana peels, where I learned about banana peels? And why a banana, of all fruits? What is it that excites our cause-creating drive? A kind of *nervus sympathicus?* But that banana, the shape of it, the obviousness of it. But, of course, some are more *banana* than are others, a sort of general formula for embarrassment. Wouldn't you say, Townsend?

Nietzsche

Freud

INFLATO: Douglas, please.

MO: Here's your wine, Professor Barthes.

INFLATO: I've been trying to perform semiological analysis on the film *Lawrence of Arabia* and it hasn't been going well.

BARTHES: You must first accept the structural pitfalls of gestural language and realize how, shall we say, impotent the hand of

---

15. My lack of familiarity at the time with Balzac's novella perhaps hindered my ability to be fair in reading *S/Z,* but just because one doesn't see the shit in the toilet doesn't mean one does not smell it. I perceived a claim in the text to point out the remarkable fertility of language, but, in the text, the very practice of language seemed to work like radiation on testes. The threat of epiphany was large and used to hold me hostage, the man telling me that if I stopped reading it was because I was inflexible and a slave to common thinking and forcing me to feel like a simple-minded disciple with each word deeper into the text, until the end when I threw the book out of my crib, and laid a load in my big-boy underwear.

Twain	the director, not only is, but must be. This in order to allow the film the room it needs for the kind of attention I need to give it. And the particular movie you mention, why it has no clutter of cultural signs, despite its pretense. The function of the signs is in tacit conspiracy with the subverted language in all games of discourse and that is, of course, the final blow to the director.

Don't you agree?

INFLATO: Yes.

MO: Why don't we move into the other room for dinner?

Mo lifted me from my playpen and carried me to the table. As she strapped me into my high chair, she whispered, "I hope you're not as bored as I am." I nodded, but she didn't see it. I looked at the cigarette dangling from Barthes' fingers. He did not notice my staring. I don't think he was aware of my presence.

MO: We're having pork butt. I hope you eat meat.

INFLATO: Some months ago I sent you an off-print of my paper on alterity. It was in *Critical Inquiry.*

BARTHES: Christian eschatology appears in two forms, one personal, the other cosmic. When a person dies, it's like a world ending.[16] But what is an ending, except for a narrative device, a trick of language that would have one accept the distances between sounds and the signs representing them, between denotation and connotation. A spectrum exists with me at one end and unformed matter at the other and in between, just as before, is all sense and nonsense. Everything and nothing are ontological. The closer to me an idea gets, the less sense it makes because of its distance from its refractory origin. I call the distance *infinite privation.*

Aquinas

Searle

---

16. The idea snapped me awake and I was shocked to find myself not only understanding a word or two but in agreement. It however served only to give me a trail of thought to pursue. My mind turned to the ancient Mesopotamians and how, for them, the cosmos was always shattering without warning, only to be rebuilt and suffer another cataclysm. I wondered if dying was like the cosmos shattering or coming finally together.

INFLATO: The article was in a green envelope.

BARTHES: Evil is a privation of sorts, a lack of goodness, just as
emptiness is a lack of that which would make a void full
Miller or complete. But when a man and a woman decide that
language is simply skin and they rub it against one another, then the privation becomes something else again.
Imagine that words had fingers and we talked and
Plato achieved a kind of double contact. Wouldn't that negate
privation? Wouldn't it have to? Unless, of course, one believes in evil love.

I looked up because of what I had heard, but my parents were so per-
plexed as to be dumbfounded. They stared at their plates and pushed pork
butt and string beans around. But Barthes was looking at my mother with
his French accent.

BARTHES: Townsend, about your article.

INFLATO: Yes?

BARTHES: I haven't read it.

vita nova

The Sternum

Level,
centerpiece of the table
of my chest,
find the median line,
locate my heart.

Oblique in inclination
from above and downward,
forward,
it is my shield.

Convex on anterior
surface from side

21

to side, concave
from above
and downward.

Manubrium,
gladiolus,
ensiform,
come together,
absorb the world
through compact tissue.

degrees

I have endeavored, rather rudely perhaps, to trace the genealogy of the sickness that infected my father, and so my parents, and so my family, and so me. To view the sickness as it existed, I think, does not entail naming it, for to name it would be to miss the point and, more importantly, to limit appreciation of its effects by limiting our perceived possibilities. So, I will speak of a thing unnamed and address it as the multitude of things that it must be, keeping in mind that as I write, the thing has already undressed and changed its antigenic costume, leaving me stuck with language, with sense only in a context that no longer exists.

My father's father was a bowler. I know of the game only what I read in one article in a postmodern journal that claimed the game was an elaborate metaphor for the male-female and male-male (but not the female-female) relationship, the pins having something to do with epidermal boundaries and balls. Grandpa was a bowler, this I know because every photograph that I ever saw of him—he died during a tornado in Indiana in the late sixties—depicted him in a shirt, ugly even in black and white, which had short sleeves a darker color than the rest of it, and he was wearing similarly colored shoes with the number 9 tattooed boldly on their sides. Even in the photographs, I could see the disdain for the man on my father's face. In one picture, the back of the photo said, "Elkhart, 1955," my father's father was pretending to use his son's head as a bowling ball on his approach to the lane. The man was smiling largely. The boy looked tortured and in his eyes was not fear, but hatred. I believe the man, his name was Elton, worked in a musical-instrument factory, but had no aptitude for music himself. From things my father told my mother, he had no aptitude, no interest, and no idea that music existed outside the selections on the jukebox at the neighborhood lanes. My father pretended to love music, listening to the *right* kinds of music and memorizing the *important* works, but his interest was superficial, in spite of the breadth of his knowledge. He would listen to Mahler's *Kindertotenlieder* and no tears would come to his eyes. He would simply walk over and flip the vinyl disc. He would put on Coltrane's *My Favorite Things,* but would not become agitated or angry. Music never made him cry and it only made him smile when he purchased a difficult-to-find recording. He collected many jazz recordings and knew all the dates and all the personnel on each disc, but he felt nothing; I could see as he listened, stretched out on the sofa with his pipe or sitting in the recliner with a glass of cognac. In most things, no doubt sex among them, he confused enthusiasm with passion. He was a sort of involuntary ascetic. Like the Orfic, life in this world for Inflato was finally pain and weariness. He was passionate insofar as he was at war with himself. On the other hand, his intellect was more form than substance, a flash of style more than a deep well (no wonder the attraction to certain so-called schools of thought). Inflato imagined that he possessed a kind of control over his passions; as true as my having control over satyrs and muses. My father was not ugly, but neither was he handsome, and finally, a lack of handsomeness is a kind of ugliness, but this did not bother him, to hear him tell it, because Socrates was ugly. He would stand in front of the mirror and say to my mother, who was still drying after her shower, "In the *Symposium,* it is said that Socrates had a stumpy nose and a protruding belly." He would say no more, but leave my mother and, unknowingly, me, to infer his meaning.

mundus intelligibilis

WITTGENSTEIN: Friedrich, let me ask you a question. Do you think that my having consciousness is a fact of experience?

NIETZSCHE: Terrible experiences pose the riddle whether the person who has had them is not terrible. Who has not, for the sake of his good reputation, sacrificed himself once?

WITTGENSTEIN: If I know it solely from my own case, then of course I know only what *I* call that, not what anyone else does. Make the following experiment: say, "I have a good reputation" and *mean,* "I have a bad one." Can you do that? And what are you doing as you do it?

NIETZSCHE: What is the matter with you?

WITTGENSTEIN: Can you do it?

NIETZSCHE: Why should I want to?

WITTGENSTEIN: Then consider the following form of expression: "The number of hairs in my ears is equal to a root of the equation $x^3 + 2x - 3 = 0$." Or: "I have n friends and $n^2 + 2n + 2 = 0$."

NIETZSCHE: You are truly mad. You know, the thought of suicide is a powerful comfort: It helps one through many a dreadful night.

anfractuous

Inflato was giggling. He was holding me in his arms as he stood in the first room of the graduate student Laura's apartment. He talked a lot about how he really shouldn't be there and how it was awkward, "what with the baby and all." Then she touched his hand. He gave me a glance as if to put to me the question: Do you know what the hell is going on? I put back to him silently: No, do you?

Then he let Laura hold me. She was soft enough and I understood on some level the attraction he felt, but still I was upset by the gesture. Had I liked my father more, perhaps I could have been a bit more tolerant or even forgiving, accepting his transgression, if you will, as a human search for something. But knowing him as I did, as the man who still assigned me to periods in my playpen prison because of his belief in my retardation, as a man driven mainly by insecurity and adherence to form, I could not. What was going on was all too obvious and I felt some sadness for the naive Laura. I didn't know, however, if they had indeed already done that thing about which I had read, which caused adults so much consternation, which my parents did, and which made me, the putting of the penis into the vagina. I looked for clues, but saw none.

"I've applied for a job in Texas," my father said. "I haven't told Eve, however."

"Don't you think you should?" Laura asked, holding his hand now.

"She's happy here. It would be so hard for her to pick up everything and start over. You know, her painting and everything."

"It must be so difficult for you."

"I'm so tired of this department. Just a bunch of stodgy old farts."

Laura stroked his knuckles.

To their credit they did not go beyond knuckle fondling in front of me, but I have no doubt that later, when Inflato claimed to be in the library, he was in fact putting his penis into Laura's vagina. Had I any money, I would have bet on it.

ootheca

Out of me came a story that I presented to my mother. There had already been several poems and a few notes, and so she did not faint. She liked it and told me so, and then she read it to me. In spite of the fact that speech was so hard on my ears, I did not mind hearing it as much as I expected.

The story came after my reading of Twain's *Roughing It* and all of Zane Grey. Not a bad story, not a deep story, but a story nonetheless, decidedly more self-conscious than Twain or Grey[17] and finally not as funny as Twain and not nearly as exciting as Grey. But the story was instructive.

Mo saw the story's instructive possibility in a different way. She handed the pages to my father in my presence. He read, gave a ridiculing laugh, and said, "I don't know why you insist on keeping this joke going, but at least write a decent story."

Mo looked at me and I could feel a reaction showing in my baby face.

"Even a mildly retarded child should be able to write better than this," he said. He threw his head back, laughing. He was attempting to insult my mother, which was bad enough, but to say that about *my* story was too much. Then he said, "Mixolydian is even misspelled."

Ignorant bastard! Mo was prepared and waiting just for this. She had left a marker and notebook in the pen with me and before I knew what was happening I had taken up both. It wasn't until I was near done writing that I looked up to see the completely stunned and befuddled face of Inflato floating over me. What I wrote:

1) **Mixolydian is not misspelled.**
2) **Though the writing is young and, perhaps, overly exuberant, the story is solid and thoroughly and absolutely readable.**
3) **Da-da is full of shit.**[18]

---

17. Please forgive the mention of the two in the same breath, but understand that even then I understood their missions to be different (though not so different as one might imagine) and both to be equally successful. Of course, I lacked the wit and cynicism (the two being functions of experience) of Twain and the charming naiveté of Grey (for this lack I cannot account).

18. A term and use I discovered reading Ishmael Reed.

Inflato looked at my eyes and then to Mo, swayed for a second, then fainted. His head made a thump when it hit the carpet.

tubes 1 ... 6

During the Second World War submarines terrorized the north Atlantic. Unsuspecting ships would be suddenly struck by steam-driven torpedoes, then sink to the bottom of the ocean, never seeing their attackers. But the submarines could stay submerged for only so long and then their batteries would fail and they would have to surface to recharge while running their diesel engines. My father was the unsuspecting tanker and I was the stealthy U-boat. My mother had somehow gotten him onto the sofa and was gently bringing him around. It wasn't so much that I was afraid (what could he do to me?), but I wanted to dive, to make a couple of zigzags on my way to just beneath the layer, reduce my speed to a crawl, and creep away slowly. Who knows what was leaking out of the hole my torpedo had made in him? As he came to and focused on me, he tried to climb over the back of the sofa to get away. Mo told him to calm down.

"Calm down? The boy's a freak."

"Ralph is no freak. He's our son. And he's special. Ralph is a genius."

"He's the devil."

"I've been giving him books and he reads them. He devours them. He doesn't seem to sleep. He reads two, sometimes three books overnight." Mo was smiling at me.

"Why didn't you tell me about this?"

"I tried, but you wouldn't listen. I showed you his poem."

"This is just so unbelievable." Inflato grabbed his head and squeezed it between his palms. "Ralph is a genius," he said, staring at me. "He's not retarded."

"No, he's not," my mother laughed.

"So, what do we do?"

Mo shrugged.

"He understands everything I say?" Inflato asked.

"He certainly does. In fact, he's remarkably sophisticated. He has read Fitzgerald and Proust and Wright, and not only understands but comments on the novels in his notes."

I could see, as I stared into my father's eyes, that he was recalling my presence at his visit to Laura's apartment. He smiled weakly at me and said, "Ralph. Ralphy. Son. My child." He came around the sofa and knelt in front of me. "Daddy loves you. Do you understand? I'm so excited to find out about your . . ." he searched for the word, ". . . talent. Daddy and Mommy love you very much. Do you understand?"

"He understands, Douglas," my mother said. "He understands more than we do. I don't know what to do with him."

Inflato stood and assumed the posture of taking over. "First we have to have a doctor take a look at him."

"He's not sick," Mo said.

"A psychologist, Eve. Maybe a psychologist can tell us what's going on with him, how smart he is, and what we should do."

I put my hands out, asking for my notebook. Mo handed it to my father and he handed it, cautiously, to me. I wrote:

Ralph knows a secret

I could see a single, glistening bead of perspiration break out of his ample forehead. And behind the bead I could see the wheels turning, slowly at first and then even more slowly. I obliterated my message with my marker and watched him exhale a sigh of relief, but our understanding had been established.

donne lieu

Everyone speaks of Thucydides, but Xenophon is dismissed as less than brilliant. But it is exactly his lack of brilliance that should have us remember him. His plainness is beautiful. His limitations are precise and astonishing. The *Oeconomicus,* a sort of codicil to the *Memorabilia,* is a remarkable work of mediocrity, but we still read it some 2,300 years later. What better subject for a student of Socrates to direct his scrutiny than the training of a housewife? Time has been kind and generous in its treatment of Xenophon's substantial oeuvre. But generosity and stamina make the work no more than average and so, average work holding little or no value and interest for me, I consider the man and what stands out is his dullness. At dullness he excels. The perfect dim star. The candle beside which others are called bright. There is no substitute for the Xenophons of the world, the plodding constants, the droning, fixed designations that allow comparison and measurement. My father was such a rule and perhaps the world will remember him as a philosopher and critic, but his dullness was so profound as to be blinding. Even in dullness there must be some moderation; call it the exercise of taste. But his dullness was in excess, honed to razor bluntness, a burning monotony, a dazzling torpidity. However, and even then at thirteen months I was tortured by the thought, I was his son and I had to wonder what kind of awful genetic inevitabilities awaited me later in life. This finally is the central terror. That cytosine, thymine, adenine, and guanine and their tautomers can combine variously with bad and predictable results is sobering at least. Conscious thinking, however, I decided, might well serve to undo some of nature's doings, my having discovered the possible inevitabilities at an early enough age to employ a kind of adaptive economy. So, I had a headstart in warding off the genetic pitfalls of my ancestry, but I was physically exactly where I should have been, my brain and nervous system incapable of modulating the actions of my unformed muscles. Yes, somehow my fingers, hands, and wrists were advanced enough for the complex operation of writing, but I was pretty much helpless in all other matters physical and material and so, I was at the mercy of my parents to take care of the business of life-function maintenance. This was the second terror.

Mo loved me. Of that fact I was certain and so I could trust her to see to my needs. And Inflato was afraid of me.

umstände

The basic steps of the ontological argument for the existence of god are easily described:

    a) assume: a being such that none greater can be conceived does not exist.

    b) a being such that none greater can be conceived is not a being such that none greater can be conceived.[19]

    c) therefore: a being such that none greater can be conceived exists.

---

19. I, of course, have left to tacit implication the required assumption that existence is better than nonexistence; an unintelligible claim, but I'm willing to allow it in spite of my failure to understand it. In fact, I have no opinion concerning the existence of god. I am not an atheist, since I do not express a belief that there is no god. I am not a theist, as I do not hold the belief there is one. I am not an agnostic because I do not profess ignorance and so an inability to answer the question. I simply do not care, and so I might incorrectly (however justifiably) be identified as a twentieth-century fundamentalist Protestant or a nineteenth-century Mountain Meadows Massacre Mormon or a Catholic from any century.

That's it. I will not quarrel with the argument, offer objections to its form, premises, implicit assumptions, or its mission. I will only ask that you entertain further:

> a) assume: Ralph does not exist.
> b) **Ralph is not Ralph.**
> c) therefore: **Ralph exists.**

This was what I wrote on a nice stiff sheet of pink paper while seated on a turquoise blanket on the floor of the psychologist's office at the University Hospital. She had been pleasant and indulgent of my parents up until the time I used my father's fountain pen to begin my message to her. Then she became nervous and animated and suggested numerous times that it was all a trick and that obviously I had superior, abnormally superior, motor skills, but insisted that I couldn't possibly know what I was doing. And so I added in a crude, childlike scribble:

what does shrinkie want ralph to do?

The doctor, a very tall woman named Steimmel, looked at me and screamed something unintelligible, then looked at my parents and screamed again. She excused herself and returned just less than a minute later.

"Well, Mr. and Mrs. Townsend, shall we sit down and talk?" Steimmel asked. "I'll have one of the nurses watch Ralph."

My father glanced at me and I gave a quick shake of my head to show my disapproval. Inflato said, "I'd like Ralph to stay with us."

"Mr. Townsend, I think it's better if—"

"No, I want him here," Inflato said.

My mother questioned him by saying his name.

"Ralph wants it," he whispered loud enough for everyone to hear.

"Ralph wants it?" Steimmel repeated his words.

Mo looked at me and asked me, "Do you want to remain in here with us?"

I nodded.

"You don't really believe he understands what's going on?" asked Steimmel. The woman was staring at me like I was on fire and so I rolled my eyes as I had seen my mother do when talking with my father. Steimmel looked away, then sat down on the sofa across the room.

The conversation that ensued was full of furtive and not-so-furtive glances over toward the baby in question. It began with the Amazon Steimmel saying, "Your son is, shall we say, *special.*"

"We know that," Mo said.

"Well, Ralph is a little more than what we usually mean when we say *special*. I'd like to run some tests, both physical and intelligence. Do you have any problem with that?"

Mo and Inflato looked over at me and I shrugged.

"I guess not," Inflato said.

Steimmel was not as inept as I presumed as she looked Inflato in the face and said, "Are you for some reason intimidated by your son?"

And it turned out that Inflato was quicker than I had given him credit for being, because he responded, "No more so than you."

Mo nodded, then said to get things on track, "It's not just the writing. Like I told you, he reads. He reads everything." She opened her bag and pulled out a stack of pages. "Here are the notes he writes to me. He dissects arguments in scholarly texts. He comments on the structure of novels. He also writes poems. He wrote a story, but I don't understand it." Saying it was hard for her, she then paused to pinch the bridge of her nose. "Is there anything wrong with my child?"

Steimmel looked through my notes. Her face registered her plummet deeper into terror. "You're sure he wrote these?"

"Positive."

Steimmel was silent for a few seconds. "And he has never spoken?"

"Not a word."

"Any sounds at all?"

"He cried for the first week or so when he was hungry," my mother said.

"Then he started pointing," Inflato said, appearing to be confronted with the information for the first time himself. "I didn't even know what he was doing. I just thought his hand was flying around. But he was pointing."

"That's true," my mother said.

Steimmel got up and walked over to her desk, regaining some composure and control, and looked at her appointment book. "Can you bring him here tomorrow morning at nine?"

My parents said they could.

I don't know what possessed Steimmel at that point, but she knelt down on the turquoise blanket beside me and said in a baby voice, "You're a sweet wittle thing, aren't you? Doctor Steimmel will see wittle Ralphie tomorrow. Okay?"

I looked away from her to my parents. It was she at whom they were staring.

mary mallon

My babiness aside, there was and is nothing *wrong* with me. Nothing about me functions improperly or incorrectly or fails to function. If anything, a couple of things worked too well, but, of course, there was the problem. If the boat knows two speeds, stop and fast, docking becomes a difficult and perhaps impossible task. One could cut the engines and drift in, but there is little control and currents can play loose with the mission and those on the pier will just hate to see you coming. I wanted, still want, and expect to continue wanting a slower gear for my brain. I cannot even say that I am smart, only that my brain is engaged in constant and frantic activity. Mo and Inflato touched me when I was an infant as if I were a container of erosive or caustic or potentially explosive material. They would race to walk away, trying to force the other to have to lift me and bring me along. Still, I know that they did not want to leave me. Mo loved me. Both were doomed by a sense of duty and societal pressure and a basic fear of doing something wrong to keep me with them and to not put me into a sack with a brick and drop me into a lake. Often, however, I found comfort in that very thought. The idea of my drowning made me more interesting to myself. I hated the helplessness, the doorknobs so far above my head, not being able to completely trust my sphincter muscles. I was constantly afraid that some adult would fry me in a skillet. Frying is very much like hunting. The unsuspecting prey is startled by the sudden heat of attack and as I saw myself as likely prey, tender, helpless, small enough to carry back to the cave, I feared for my life. My only bad dream was discovering myself in a cast-iron pan, sitting in sizzling butter. But even in the dream, I simply lay back and tried to feel the fear for all it was and sought complete silence and absence of sensation. The dream, though bad in the beginning, did not awake me with a start, as I have read happens, but became an intense, but welcome immersion into sublime pain and finally stillness. However, I caution the reader to not rush to some assumption about my wanting death or hating life in an attempt to understand me. Occam's razor is sharp and I am not afraid to use it. In fact, attempts at filling in my articulatory gaps with a kind of subtext, though it might prove an amusing exercise, will uncover nothing. At the risk of sounding cocky, my gaps are not gaps at all, but are already full, and all my meaning is surface.[20] My parents watched me read and take notes, sitting on the sofa,

---

20. If for no other reason than my having claimed it.

pretending to read themselves, but studying me all the while. During those gaps in time when my eyes were not on a book and my hand not set to writing (i.e., when I was thinking), they would sit up straight as if feeling the initial trembling of an earthquake. I did not like the effect I had on them and I regretted having allowed them knowledge of my capacities. They thought I was a genius and this I found laughable. I reserved that designation for someone who could drive a car or at least hold his shit. But I was going to go ahead with the trifling tests and I had no doubt that I could come out smelling like a great mind, true or no. That I could and would live with, and from there on I would do what I wanted and devil take the hindmost. I knew that I was headed for the battlefield and I knew what the enemy looked like and how they dressed, but I didn't yet know what any of our weapons would be.

Jhem or Shem

Knowledge of my ability to see the world caused my father to act as if he were the drunken Noah at the end of the ark's voyage and I, Ham. But there were no Shem and Japheth to hide his nakedness. So, whereas I still caught a occasional glimpse of my mother's breasts, I never again saw my father's willy. Nor did my father ever again bathe me. My willy, on the other hand, was still of interest to me and I learned that I could change its attitude. At first I thought I had broken the thing, but a bit of reading cleared up the matter.

No Children are Volunteers. Therefore, no children being tested by Psychologists are volunteers—

$$(x)(Cx \rightarrow \sim Vx) \vdash (x)[(Cx \& Px) \rightarrow \sim Vx]$$

Statius, in the eighth book of the *Thebaid* describes how after Menalippus mortally wounded Tydeus in the war of the Seven against Thebes, Tydeus was still able to kill Menalippus. The interesting part is when Menalippus' head was brought to Tydeus, Tydeus chewed on it like a big apple in a fit of rage. I cannot decide whether Tydeus was so outraged because his opponent had taken his life or because Menalippus had done such a poor job and allowed his dying to drag out so.

exousai

The sounds of the hospital were what I expected, whispering, the rolling of carts, the unrhythmic buzzing from this way and that, and an infrequent cackle from a nurse or doctor and that is what I heard until my presence was detected. Word spread like airborne pheromones and then all on the floor was silent, all available eyes turned to me and a few previously absent pairs appeared around the corners of doorways. Steimmel met us outside her office. She was not wearing her khaki skirt showing beneath her lab coat that day, but a pair of demin trousers and a loose-fitting sweater, as if she expected a fight or, at least, to get down on the floor and wrestle.

"Professor and Mrs. Townsend," she greeted my parents and then to me, with the same insipid baby-chat she'd ended our last time together, she said, "And how is wittle Ralph doing?"

Mo, sensing my mood, asked, "Can we just get started?" She adjusted my weight on her side.

"Certainly. If you two would just take seats in the waiting area over there, I'll take Ralph in for the first test."

Inflato moved to protest.

"Please, Professor Townsend. I assure you everything will be just fine."

My mother looked at me and I gave her a covert wink. She then handed me over to the hard and awkward hands of the doctor.

Steimmel took me into a room with tiny furniture obviously meant for child a few years older than me and sat me at a tiny table. "Okay, young man," she said, stepping to the large mirror across the room, then walking back to me. "Let's see what you can do." She took a tray from a cabinet and put it in front of me. "Boy, do I feel stupid saying this to you, but, why don't you put the blocks here into the right holes."

I looked at her and frowned, then shrugged.

She turned to the mirror and said, "A learned gesture, no doubt. Not much more than a tick. Go."

The eight holes were filled with circles, squares, rectangles, and triangles before her lips had closed from saying the "o" in go. I looked up at her wide brown eyes. Then I dumped the pieces out onto the table and did it again as quickly.

"Well, okay." She paused as if to compose herself, then said to the mirror, "As I mentioned, the child exhibits extraordinary motor skills." Then to me, "Repeat after me."

I shook my head. Then I gestured that I wanted paper and something with which to write. She went back to the cabinet and returned with a pad and a marker, put them in front of me.

"Q," she said. I didn't write. I knew she wanted to give me a string of things and so I waited. Then, as if accepting a challenge, she fired off, "Q, seven, T, Q, V, B, N, Q, thirteen."

I wrote down the letters and spelled out the numbers.

Steimmel gasped. Then, double rapid-fire, "T, U, K, six, Y, Y, Y, A, I, E, Y, Y, Y, Y, X, D, J, K, J, L, two, two, Y, Y, Y, Y, I."

I wrote down what she had said.

"Okay," she said and now she was pacing, to the mirror and back to me. "The subject appears to have an excellent memory. We'll try something crazy here." She pointed at me. "Two plus two."

4

"Three times seven."

21

"Two hundred seventy-six divided by thirty-three."

8.36363636363636 . . .

"Solve for x, 3x equals thirty-nine."

x=13

Steimmel went to the cabinet and took out a book. "All right, you little bastard," she said. She read: "'If a plane area is revolved about a line that lies in its plane but does not intersect the area, then the volume generated is equal to the sum of the area and the distance traveled by its center of gravity.' Can you make any sense of that?" Steimmel was perspiring, casting desperate glances at the mirror. She appeared unsteady on her feet.

**1st theorem of Pappus. And may I point out that it is
the product and not the sum of the area and the distance traveled
by its center of gravity.[21]**

Steimmel snatched the pad from my wittle hands and threw it across the room as hard as she could. I watched her and, though, I didn't show it,

---

21. This is was a lucky stroke, as I had just read about the theorems of Pappus. I would have been unable to provide a proof for the first theorem and I would not have recognized the second.

I was more than a tiny bit frightened by her hysterics. She went to the mirror and screamed at her reflection. Then she went to the door and screamed for my parents.

derivative

Pothen to kakon
bene ha-elohim
mal'ak Yahweh
onomata
angeloi
Nergal

incision

My parents and Steimmel and the people who had been hidden behind the mirror huddled like plotters in a corner across the room, each one in turn raised his or her head to check on my whereabouts. They were all so frightened, though the quality of my mother's fear was discernibly different. I wanted her to break away from the group, lift me, and take me home.

"It's not possible," Steimmel said in a voice not a whisper.

A short, balding man with thick glasses worked away on a calculator, then grabbed his head, shaking it at the same time. "Four seventy-five," he said.

A husky woman wearing a brown suit said, "I get the same thing."

"Not possible," Steimmel said.

Mo and Inflato looked over at me with their mouths agape. "Four seventy-five?" Inflato asked. "Good lord."

Steimmel took over and said, "If all of you would excuse me, I would like to talk to Ralph alone. Just everybody, just step outside." She ushered them toward the door and closed them out, then turned to face me, fear showing in her eyes, but her movements suggesting that she had remembered that she was much larger and stronger than me. "Okay, young man, let's get down to some real business here." She went to the cabinet and came back with a thick folder. She sat in one of the tiny chairs near me. "I want you to look at some pictures for me. Here, now, tell what you see in this one."

I wrote:

It reminds me of Motherwell's
Elegy to the Spanish Republic No. 70.[22]

I could see that my answer distressed her and so I wrote:

I think I see a bear. Is that a bear dere. Ouch, bear bite me.

Steimmel snatched back the blot. "You're a smart ass." Then she sat and just stared at me. "I don't know what to do," she said to herself. "I don't understand any of this."

Mo burst into the room and marched over to me. "Come on, Ralph, we're going home."

subjective-collective

I slept little, but when I did, my dreams were vivid and of a kind. I was hardly ever present in them in a capacity other than spectator. They were like the novels my mother fed me constantly. Some were like tone poems, but with images, not lacking narrative impetus, but straining the convention. Indeed, I wondered as I read more and more about dreams, in fiction and in psychoanalytic literature, about the convention of dream narrative, as it seemed that all descriptions of dreams fit a rather narrowly defined picture. Interpretation, of necessity, is of interest to anyone who hears the story of a dream, but my interest became the structure of, not any specific dream, but of the category. "That's sounds like a dream." "It was like a dream." "It must have been a dream."

So, imagining that I had exposed the tricks of dream convention, I sought, consciously at least, to subvert the whole thing and dream in as straight a narrative fashion as possible. My dreams frequently became movies, without bizarre logical twists, every action and word making sense even upon my waking. My dreams became so transparent that they became devoid of meaning. Jung would have been proud of me. Freud would have gone to sleep during our sessions. My dreams became an exercise in boredom, though I was actually impressed with my imagination and its

---

22. I, in fact, was slightly pained that I could not come up with a painting, the title of which might have had significant import for the situation. The fact of the matter was that the blot looked just like that painting, moving me as much, meaning as little. Not a knock on Motherwell at all, however. I love his *Pancho Villa, Dead and Alive,* the colors, the shapes, the composition, the vacuity.

ability to create so many characters, even if they were stock and repetitive. I thought I knew how it felt to be Louis L'Amour or James Michener or even Dickens.

Ironically, the actuality of my having subverted my dreaming practice made the fact of my dreaming of great interest. I wondered what indeed it meant about me that I was so set against the notion of convention that I should attack it. So, I replaced the *dream* with the *novel,* stripping the stories of my dreams of any real meaning, but causing the form of them to mean everything.[23]

---

23. And so, I assume, nothing, as no thing can actually mean everything.

A Plot with a View

secondary sign:
    metalanguage

$$\text{expression}_2 \quad (R_2) \quad \text{content}_2$$

primary sign: object language

$$\text{expression}_1 \ (R_1)$$
$$\text{content}_1$$

BARTHES

B

différance

What troubled my parents and Dr. Steimmel wasn't so much that I understood language, but that I basically understood it as they did. It was clear, at least to me, that they suffered from a kind of jealousy, the nature of which remains unclear, but it concerned my having skipped what Steimmel would have wanted to call a symbolic or imaginary stage in my development, a prelinguistic rite of passage, a necessary inconvenience during which they expected to have enormous influence. But my thinking was *organized;* the time during which I was to roughly come to understand the delimiting of my body I used to form a personality, changing, as we always are changing, but knowing more than the parts of my body and their relations. Indeed, the claim might be made that because I lacked the prelinguistic clutter, the subtextual litter, I actually understood language better than any adult. Talk of time never threw me for a loop. Pronouns never confused me. I used *me* when I was supposed to and never once wondered when my mother used *I* whether she was speaking of me. *You, me, they, them, it, she, he* all did their work without baffling me for a second. What is more, the gap between the *subject of enunciation* and the *subject of enunciating*[1] not only failed to appear to me as a place of entry, but also failed to register as something I might elide. For me, there was no gap, as there is no gap for anyone.

---

1. This *gap* talk I discovered at the same time I determined I was a Romantic. Not because I needed to position myself as a subject of derision by the likes of my father, but because I'm fond of a good story.

bridge

My parents stopped at a restaurant on our way home from the hospital and ate in awkward silence. They looked at me only occasionally and then only for a second, offering half-meant smiles. They talked a lot about how their food was only mediocre and finally, my mother said, "I don't like that Dr. Steimmel. I don't trust her."

Inflato shrugged. "She got a little worked up, I guess."

"A little worked up? It seemed to me like she was taking things awfully personally for somebody who's supposed to remain clinical and objective."

"Nobody can be objective," Inflato said.

"You know what I mean." Mo was irritated now and so she looked to me for more than a second. "You know what I mean, don't you, Ralph?"

I nodded. Then I gestured that I wanted something to write on. Mo dug into her purse while Inflato glanced nervously around.

"My god, Eve," he said. "What if somebody sees?"

"To hell with them," Mo said. She put a pad and a pen in front of me. I wrote:

I don't want to go back to the hospital.

Mo read it and told Inflato what I had said. "Don't worry honey, we won't take you back there."

"Maybe not there," Inflato said. "Eve, we have to get some answers, learn what we need to do to deal with him."

"*Him* is sitting right here. It's not like he's got a contagious disease, Douglas."

"How do we know?"

I felt my little body convulsing with laughter. I wrote:

Father *wishes* I were contagious.

Mo read it and laughed.

Inflato grabbed the pad and read it. "Very funny. So, you're smart, you little nipple-hound."

I wrote quickly:

So, that's it, you're jealous of the attention your wife pays me.

He pulled the pad over, read it, and bit his lip. "That's not it. You need special help. I don't want you to grow up all twisted inside. You could become a juvenile delinquent or worse."

A poststructuralist pretender.

That one really scared him. He ate a forkload of potato salad and looked away. I was not proud of having stepped on him the way I did, but I was interested in the exchange because it was my first real confrontation. Certainly, I had toyed with Steimmel and watched her lose her grip, but with my father at the table, I actually felt a twinge of anger. I learned at that table that I had a mean streak.

anfractuous

Whether atoms, monads, or words, things are made up of small things and small things are made of smaller things and, to some extent, my understanding of the whole world depends on my comprehension of its constituent parts. But my poop is my poop, to me here in California, to a fat Australian woman in Melbourne, to an engineer in Nigeria, to a pearl diver in the South Pacific. And though Inflato might have argued to the contrary, my performance at the shrink's was limited to a finite number of readings. He would, in his philosophical mode, have liked to claim an infinite number of interpretations, but as is the case with most *theories,* application is a bit of a sticky wicket. Locke might have claimed all day that there was no material world, but still he would have stepped out of the way of an oncoming carriage that evening.

An infinite number of readings indeed. Certainly, my sentences read backwards or pulled from the text randomly will produce the kind of *fragments* certain individuals have suggested. I am free to read this way. But I do not, any more than I might walk the middle part of my trip to the refrigerator first this time and last the next. Even when I have read half the novel, when I go back and read the first lines of the first chapter, I am reading the beginning. If I could, I would make numerous trips to the refrigerator. Sometimes I would be hungrier than others. Sometimes I would retrieve a bottle of milk, others, strained peaches. Still, it would be a trip to the refrigerator that begins at my little desk. Even if I were just going there to feel the cold air on my face, it would be a trip to the refrigerator. Never would I go there to see an elephant.

ens realissimum

G.E. MOORE: Imagine that we are characters in your story *Sarrasine* and that you know the truth about La Zambinella while I do not. Do we see the same thing when we see him come into the room?

45

BALZAC: You mean to say that I know La Zambinella is a castrato dressed as a woman and you do not.

G.E. MOORE: That is correct.

BALZAC: Well, we both see La Zambinella.

G.E. MOORE: But do we see the same La Zambinella?

BALZAC: We see her femininity and her station and her clothes and I have her appear as a kind of apparition. Are you asking if we see those things?

G.E. MOORE: Not exactly. You see a man in women's clothes. I see a woman.

BALZAC: But we both see La Zambinella.

G.E. MOORE: But you see so much more than I.

BALZAC: I know more and perhaps I am aware of more. I can find and entertain certain ironies that you cannot, but I see the same Zambinella as you.

G.E. MOORE: But how can you, if you're seeing with your mind and I am seeing with mine?

BALZAC: That is a different question.

seme

Fissure of Sylvius

Where in my head
do the breaches meet,
defining the parietal lobe
from the temporal?

Sylvius joining Rolando
at the tortured frontal,
where the crying starts,
where the crying stops.

Beginning in a depression,
an interior,
perforated space

situated within,
it moves out of the hemisphere,

pushes forward
a limb,
a short ascending finger,
upward,
inward into the frontal
convolution.

ephexis

What I know of my parents' lives I know from photographs. I know some-what more about my mother's life now, but, generally, people are only in-clined to speak of the past with those they believe will somehow not only share some commonality, but who will also be disposed to exhibiting sym-pathy. The photographs are many; some of their childhoods, some of their courting and marriage, but few in between.

1) My mother is eight, if my math is correct, and she is sitting on a porch with her brother Toby, I can tell by his ears, and they are looking down into Toby's lap where there is a cat.

"This cat is dying," Toby said.

"Is not," said Eve.

"Papa said he's real sick."

Eve got up from her seat beside Toby and walked to the edge of the porch. "I think it's going to snow."

"The cat is suffering, Eve."

"I hope there's no school tomorrow."

Toby put the cat down on the place where Eve had been sitting and walked over to stand behind her. "Sis, I'm sorry about your cat. I'm going to take it out back now, okay?"

"Maybe we can make a snowman in the morning."

Toby put his hand on her shoulder. "Sure thing."

2) Inflato is fourteen and standing in the background, behind his father who is posing with a fat man wearing a raccoon cap. Inflato is hold-ing an oddly shaped case that seems heavy for him.

"I'm blind," Douglas's father said, tipping his beer bottle for another swig.

"Yeah, that's some flash you got on that thing," the fat man said to the tall, skinny man who was pulling the burned bulb from the pan of the Brownie.

"You boys ready to go kick some butt?" the fat man said. "How about you, Dougie? You want be on the team with your old man?"

Douglas tried to give the bag to his father. "No, I'm going to stay home. I don't really like bowling."

The skinny man and the fat man said, "Whoa, he don't like bowling."

The skinny man said, "What gives, Tommy? Your boy queer or something?"

Douglas's father shut up the skinny man with a glare. "No, he ain't queer." Then he looked at Douglas. "You ain't queer, are you?"

Douglas didn't say anything, just put down the case.

"That ball too heavy for you, son?"

"I guess so," Douglas said.

Douglas's father turned to the fat man and the skinny man. "He's going to stay in his room and read."

"Read?"

"Read. Can you believe it?"

3) *Mo and Inflato are not married yet. They are sitting in front of a campfire. It is not quite dark and there is a lake behind them.*

"I didn't think it would be this cold up here this time of year," Douglas said. He held Eve tighter and pulled her hands under his parka.

"I don't mind," Eve said. "The fire is nice."

"I didn't expect it to be this crowded either."

Eve looked down the trail. "Where did Derrick and Wanda go?"

"They said they were going to get some more gear from the car. But I think they went to you-know-what."

Eve laughed.

"How is your painting going?"

"Not badly." She watched as Douglas put another couple of sticks on the fire. "I just finished a big canvas that kind of scares me. There's a lot of green in it. Green is tough for me. There are some places in it, though, where I could just live." She stared into the fire. "I love the paint. The smell of it. The texture." She seemed to laugh at herself. "Am I rambling?" Eve looked up at the sky, which was almost dark. "God, look at that moon."

"My article on Propp's theory of Russian fairy tales was just rejected by *Modern Literary Theory.*"

"I'm sorry."

degrees

Is a photograph always present tense? I described them so. About photos people say things like, "Here I am after nearly drowning," or "There you are with Linda Evangelista." Looking up from the photo, you might then ask, "When were you with Linda Evangelista?" I tell you I was not with her. Looking back at the photo, you say, "Here you are right here with her." So, better, let the question be, is what is in the photograph always in the present, without a before, without an after? Of course, it is. And isn't that actually *you* in the picture?

incision

I was lying in my crib, reading *Daisy Miller* when I heard sounds outside my window. I stood up and attended to the noises, wondered if my parents heard them in their room, wondered if they were outside making the noises. Choosing not to engage in speech had its drawbacks, among them an inability to summon help from the next room. As I watched the sash of my window begin to move, I considered hurling a book across the room to make a ruckus, but I was not strong enough to do it and, even if I had been that strong, I would not have found it in myself to do such a thing to a book.[2]

My window opened and in rushed the cold February air. A woman's voice whispered angrily to someone else outside. Then someone was climbing through the window into my room. Dressed in dark clothes and wearing a black knit cap was Dr. Steimmel. She put a finger to her lips as she approached my bed.

---

2. I say this even though one of the texts in my crib at the time was Harold Bloom's *A Map of Misreading.*

"Don't be scared, Ralph," she said. "This is all just a dream.[3] I'm not going to hurt you."

Another similarly dressed person was at the window, but he didn't come in. "Just grab him so we can get out of here," the man said.

"Shhhh!" Steimmel hushed him. "Come on, Ralphie." She lifted me and held me to her chest. Her bra seemed to be made of hard plastic.

"Let's go," the man at the window said.

"I'm coming, damnit." Steimmel wrapped me up in the cotton blankets of my bed and carried me to the window where she handed me to the man. He was smaller than Steimmel and, in a significant fashion, softer. The cold air, in spite of the blankets, was rude and I felt my body shiver involuntarily. The man put me under the front of his wool coat. It was scratchy, even through the layers of blanket, but warm. He stepped away from the window and let Steimmel climb out.

"You should close the window," the man said. "They might feel the cold and wake up."

"Good thinking," Steimmel said. She turned back to the house and quietly lowered the sash. "Okay, now, let's get the hell out of here. Oh, my god, I can't believe I've got him."

The man carried me and the two of them made their way across the yard, crouched low like monkeys, to a dark sedan.

Inside the car, in the dark, Steimmel strapped me into a carrier in the backseat, stuck a legal pad and a marker in front of me, and said, "Knock yourself out."

ennuyeux

On Ludwig Boltzman's tombstone is carved: $S = k. \text{Log} W$. S is the entropy of a system, k represents Boltzman's Constant, and W is a measure of the chaos of a system, essentially the extent to which energy is dispersed in the world. This equation meant little to me as I read of it the first time, but as I considered it I grew excited. The space between S and W is the space between the thing in front of me and the stuff hidden inside beyond my ob-

---

3. I was interested in her lie. What could she have thought I was working through by having such a dream? What kind of symbol could she have thought she might be for me? Perhaps she considered, even in waking life, that she be could a condensation of the world and my parents or perhaps a displacement of some adjacent influence. Whatever her delusion, she was not nearly enigmatic enough to pass for some wild hair of a symbolic image in a dream of mine.

servation and comprehension. It raises the question: How many ways can the parts of a thing be rearranged before I can see a difference? How many ways can the atoms and molecules of my hand move and recombine before I realize that something is wrong? Thinking about it scared me. Certainly, I understood that natural events symbolize collapse into chaos and that events are motivated by dissolution, but the idea of such subversive and invisible change moved me. I likened it to observing the minds of others.

mary mallon

The man with Steimmel, whose name was Boris, drove hunched over, his lips nearly touching the steering wheel. I could see him through the gap between the front seats. The sun was just coming up over the hills and we were headed north along the coast. I could smell the coffee that Steimmel was guzzling.

"I have a really bad feeling about this," Boris was saying again.

But this time Steimmel responded. She said, "Of course you have a bad feeling, you dope. We just kidnapped a kid. But it's for science. Hell, we might even be saving the planet." Steimmel laughed a hoarse laugh. "At the very least, this little bastard is going to make me famous. He's the link, Boris. He's the link between the imaginary and symbolic phases. I'm going to dissect him and then it will be Freud, Jung, Adler, and Steimmel. And to hell with Lacan. He's just Freud in an spray can."

"The kid can't be that special," Boris said.

"The fucker writes poetry. He writes stories."

"Are they any good?"

"Shut up." She turned in her seat to glance back at me. "The little worm is listening to us right now. He probably believes he understands what we're saying. Right, Ralphie?"

I wrote a note, crumpled it and tossed it in the direction of Steimmel. She found it and read:

So that I don't die of boredom back here would you explain to me what Lacan means by the sliding signified and the floating signifier?

Steimmel began to laugh wildly. "I'm going to be fucking famous. Those professors of mine back at Columbia will choke on crow now. The pigs. Boris, who is the greatest psychoanalytic thinker you know?"

"You are." Then, slightly under his breath, he added, *"Unsere letzte Hoffnung, meine Führerin."*

51

"Be careful, Boris."

I was concerned about my mother. I could see her walking into my room and finding me gone. At first, she would not believe it, then as she heard my father stirring in the bedroom, it would sink in. She would scream and my father would come running into the room and figure out what was wrong. And they would stand there holding each other, not out of love but fear, not to support but to remain standing. They would search the house, then Inflato would call the police while Mo continued the search outside in the yard and garden, maybe even moving down the street, house to house. I did not like the expression I imagined on my mother's face.

pharmakon

I knew of cinema only what I had read. I had never seen a movie, though I knew the stories of many. And I believed I understood the narrative structure of them, but there was one device that escaped me. It was the montage. And though my first example[4] of it was poorly done, I could still appreciate the possibilities, especially the camp ones. I knew that I would have to employ the technique in my dreams and even in my recollections. The montage seemed to me at the time a kind of sideways game, a parade just begging for metonymic substitutions and displacements. I entertained my mind with the construction of montage after montage while Steimmel and her lackey tried to sleep.

spacing

a) the doctor pulls me from the womb

b) my mother and father smile at each other

c) the clock on the wall registers the passage of an hour

d) my mothers is putting a question to a nurse, who gestures for her to wait

e) the doctor talks to my father in the waiting room, puts his hand on my father's shoulder

f) my father sits on the edge of my mother's bed, tells her something that makes her cry

---

4. In fact, it was my first movie, a made-for-television affair starring wooden actors and using a contrived plot, and I saw it on a motel-room television. Steimmel and Boris wanted to be off the roads during the daylight hours.

g) I am tiny and encased in glass, my little hands squeezing
   nothing, wires and tubes everywhere
h) outside, birds fly through a park and children play with
   dogs

ootheca

Ezra Pound said, "Every word must be charged with meaning to the ut-
most possible degree." Let it be the case then. But words need no help
from anyone. Bet thew ords kneeknow hellip freeum heinywon. Context,
story, time, place—don't these work like Bekins men, packing the words
like so many trunks? But finally, words are not cases to be packed at all,
but solid bricks (and, of course, like a brick, even a word's atoms are not
motionless).

exousai

Sint cadavera eorum, in escam volatilibus coeli, et bestis terrae.

To me, Steimmel and the Steimmels of the world were jackals. I grew, ir-
rationally, angry with my parents as I watched the jackal sleep. My parents
might have worshipped my bones, I thought, but my flesh they were willing to give over to wild beasts of the land. I viewed myself as dead and left
on a platform for weather and birds to tear apart.

Steimmel and Boris slept fully clothed, the doctor's dark tennis shoes
on the floor by the bed. She snored slightly and by the light from the television I could see her parted lips and her tobacco- and coffee-stained teeth.
She and her accomplice were so peaceful as to appear dead. I wondered
what might come and eat them. I thought that perhaps we would be found
and presumed dead, only to awaken and find that we had been sentenced
to the gibbet. And there, while on display for passersby to gawk at our
corpses and count our crimes, we would open our eyes and scare the life
out of all the onlookers.

> *Down the close and up the stair*
> *But and ben wi' Burke and Hare*
> *Burke's the butcher, Hare's the thief*
> *Knox's the man who buys the beef.*

supernumber

1

Only an efficient net or spray of myopia could have kept Steimmel or Boris from realizing that transporting me was going to be a conspicuous matter. Although, being a baby, I had been spared the realities of racial attitudes in the culture, my readings in genetics and history and current events made it clear that the people on the street were going to find the discrepancy between my skin color and my abductors' at least notable and perhaps worthy of some explanation.

2

Have you to this point assumed that I am white? In my reading, I discovered that if a character was black, then he at some point was required to comb his Afro hairdo, speak on the street using an obvious, ethnically identifiable idiom,[5] live in a certain part of a town, or be called a nigger by someone. White characters, I assumed they were white (often, because of the ways they spoke of other kinds of people), did not seem to need that kind of introduction, or perhaps legitimization, to exist on the page. But you, dear reader, no doubt, whether you share my pigmentation or cultural origins, probably assumed that I was white. It is not important unless you want it to be and I will not say more about it, but a physical description of one kidnapped baby would have to be released to the police and that description, being delivered by my parents, would be more or less precise and therefore, two, rather pale, white people traveling up the California coast with a baby possessing at least one of the attributes of the rendered portrait might have a problem.

3

I had never seen my parents on television. The mere sight of them moving in two-dimensional space was so compelling that I nearly missed what was being said. The caption beneath their worried faces read: Parents of the

---

5. This was particularly difficult for me to spot because I had had no experience with the outside world when first exposed to literature. All idioms and vernacular were lost on me, and so, sadly, much of the meaning, intended or otherwise. I wonder about the language of babies and realized that I didn't even have a world of babies through which to move and call my own. I was truly without a country and in that way I understand the literature of the people with whom I shared like coloration (though from what I read that coloration had extraordinary range, which seemed to go unacknowledged by what was specified as the oppressing culture).

kidnapped baby. The reporter gave my description and even put on camera a photograph of me, however unflattering, and added that I was extremely bright. I did not like seeing my picture there and as I entertained the thought that many people were seeing it also, I felt violated. But finally, what I was left with was a sick feeling because of the tears in Mo's eyes. Even Inflato's face showed grief that I found affecting.

"Do you think they know about us?" Boris asked.

"How could they?" Steimmel barked. "I told them at the office that I was taking my long overdue vacation. So, my absence is explained."

"How are we supposed to go anywhere with him?" Boris pointed to me, then crossed the room and peeked out the window at the morning sky. "It's raining. Maybe that will give us some cover or something."

"We only have a few more hours on the road and then we're home free." Steimmel started to pull off her shirt.

"What are you doing?" Boris asked.

"I'm going to take a shower. I suggest you take one, too. It'll calm you down." She finished pulling her shirt over her head and then removed her bra. Her breasts were ugly and unappetizing, though they did serve to turn my mind to food. Her nipples were very pale pink, hardly more pronounced than goose bumps, and surrounded by exaggerated areolae.

libidinal economy

Just as the good Judge Woolsey had written in his judgment of *Ulysses,* so I wrote to Boris as he sat on the bed of the motel room listening to Steimmel's shower:

The effect of Doctor Steimmel is undoubtedly somewhat emetic.

Poor Boris looked at my note. Such an expression I could not have imagined, as it became clear that, although I had written several pages in the car and a couple of notes to Steimmel, Boris did not know my secret, or at least had not believed it was true. He stared at me and began to hyperventilate, his thin lips puckering as he choked himself on his own carbon dioxide. He pulled himself to his feet and ran into the steamy bathroom, leaving the door wide open for me to see inside. I guess the steam exacerbated his problem because he fell to the floor, grabbing the shower curtain on his way down, and exposing Steimmel who was touching herself in a manner not unlike my explorations with my willy.

Steimmel let out a short scream and snapped at Boris, "What the hell are you doing?"

55

"Can't breathe, Dr. Steimmel," he gasped.

"Good lord, man," she said. "Sit up and put your head between your legs and try to breathe slowly."

Boris followed her instructions while the doctor dried her body.

"These motel towels aren't worth a fuck," she said. "Are you okay?"

Boris nodded.

"What happened?"

"That baby," he said and he pointed through the doorway at me sitting on the bed. "That baby."

"What about that baby?"

"That baby wrote me a note."

"Of course, he did. I told you he could. Why else would I want that shit machine with us?"

"I thought you meant he could make letters. But he used the word *emetic*. And quite properly, I might add."

Steimmel sucked her teeth and took a step toward me. "Yeah, the little bastard's got some fucking vocabulary. He's what I've waited my entire professional life for. Fuck Piaget."

Steimmel had some mouth on her. And it was no response to her or any of her antics, but no one had placed me for some time on the pot and I did what babies do.

"What's that smell?" Steimmel asked. She looked at Boris. "Damnit."

donne lieu

The story is told of Leibniz that he never actually gave gifts as wedding presents, but instead offered brides rules of conduct and advice, the final bit of wisdom being that the woman not give up bathing after having found a husband. He was, of course, Voltaire's Pangloss, but this Leibniz was the approval-seeking, optimistic, and shallow Leibniz and the more interesting Leibniz remained stashed in the backs of his desk drawers and under his bed. It occurred to me as I considered the man, sitting in my high chair, listening to Inflato hold forth, that the likes of my father might say that it was sad that Leibniz kept the good work under the bed. I thought that it was lamentable that the work did not remain there, safe from the ravages of fame seekers, of name builders, of dogma feeders. Tell your ideas not to talk to strangers. Don't let your ideas play in the street. Don't give your ideas any toys with pieces so small that they might choke on them.

vita nova

Pink and white oleanders lined the long drive; the rain that was falling heavily during most of the trip along the highway was now a drizzle. The wipers of the car struck a sick, intermittent cadence, hard to count and unsteeling as I contemplated just how far from my home I was. It didn't matter that I was in the same state and not on the other side of the globe. What mattered was that my mother didn't know where I was. What mattered was that my mother was clinging desperately to the hope that I was still alive, a little baby in the world of bad weather, people, and ideas. I imagined my mother wailing, sitting on the floor of the room where her child once slept, screaming unintelligible sounds through the night, disturbing the sympathetic neighbors, and exciting a few far-off coyotes. Inflato might be holding her, or standing away, leaning on the doorjamb, wanting himself to cry out, but not having the presence, the security, the lack of self-consciousness, lacking the femininity for such pure response, and wanting to help his wife but feeling lost to the task.

The drive was neat, maintained with precision, no doubt, by little professional men who came every other day in pickups held together with baling wire. The tires of the sedan kicked up pebbles and threw them wildly beneath the undercarriage. The estate, the hospital, sanitarium, criminal retreat was soft pink stucco nestled in a stand of palms. The main lodge and its outlying structures were roofed with red tiles, all the buildings showing the curves of archways and balconies. It looked like a secret place. It looked quiet and covert in spite of the several people who walked about, invidious, pernicious, sinister. I could sense in Boris an apprehension, but Steimmel was beside herself with excitement, almost bouncing in her seat.

"I've reserved three buildings for my work," she said. "The subject will sleep in the lab. We'll use the remaining two as living quarters."

"This place gives me the creeps," Boris said. "All of those turns and dirt roads. I would never have known this was here."

"That's the point, Boris. I've spent every cent I have for this secrecy. And it damn well better remain secret. Do you catch my drift?"

"Yes, Dr. Steimmel."

"That means no calls to that little girlfriend of yours. That means no calls to that little boyfriend of yours. And that especially means, no calls to your mother." Steimmel stared at him.

"I get it. I get it."

Vexierbild

Dear Bertrand,

Imagine that I ask you to take the kettle from the stove. You look over and see steam rising from its spout. It will whistle shortly. You understand my request and you walk over and remove it from the burner. If you have initiative, you will make the tea. But suppose further, that there is no kettle and that indeed there is no stove. Suppose that we are sitting at a tennis match and I say, "Would you please remove the kettle from the stove?" There are those who will claim that you understand the meaning of my words, but not the *meaning*[6] of my words. When, in fact, you do not understand anything. You might look at me and think, "Did I hear Luddy correctly?" or you might look about to see if another spectator also heard me. So, you ask, "What did you say?" and I say the same thing again. Unless you defer to me in all matters or unless you know that I have a habit of setting up a portable gas stove and making tea in inappropriate places, you will think that I have flipped my wig. You will not say to anyone that of course you know what it means to take a kettle off a stove or that you know what kettle, but you will say, "Help! My poor friend had snapped a vessel in his brain!"

Anyway, I thought I'd share that with you. Love to the wife.

Yours,

Ludwig

Dear Ludwig,

I didn't even know you liked tennis.

Yours,

Bertrand

---

6. According to Grice, to say that a speaker means a particular thing is to say that he intends to produce some effect or change in the hearer of that thing said by means of recognition of that intention. This is *non-natural meaning*. So, in fact, the meaning of "take off the kettle" at the tennis match is not so odd at all, given that it is uttered to elicit a response, even if the response is troubled concern or nervous laughter or annoyance.

tubes 1 ... 6

In the foyer of the main lodge we were met by an elderly man named Jelloffe. I was in the arms of Boris, holding my pen in one hand and propping my pad against his chest. I wrote a note:

Your name wouldn't be Smoth Ely Jelloffe, would it?[7]

The man read the note and nodded, smiling, and then he realized just who had written it. He stared at me and backed away. He backed all the way around the desk, where, without taking his eyes from me, he pushed the register forward to Steimmel.

"You can see why we're here," Steimmel said, leaning over to sign the book.

Boris hefted me to a more comfortable position. Across the large room to my left was a pink stone fireplace with gigantic matching columns. The walls were lined with pine bookcases and the floor was covered with rugs and leather sofas and chairs. Behind the desk was a staircase that was roped off with a thin chain and a sign that said *staff*.

"I hope everything is ready," Steimmel said. She was glowing, so eager to get to the work of dissecting me that she was bouncing on the balls of her ample feet.

"Yes," said Jelloffe. "We have you in buildings 3A, B, and C." He pointed to a map of the grounds on the desk. "You can park here. Just go around the building, past the stables, and it's to your right. The cottages are in a row. The library is open until midnight every night. And we would just love it if you would join us for dinners and share your findings with us."

"Ha," Steimmel said. "I'm not sharing a goddamn thing. And if I catch anybody sniffing around our area, I'll bite off his fucking head." Then she smiled. "We'd be happy to take meals with you."

$$(x)(Cx \rightarrow \sim Vx) \vdash (x)[(Cx \& Px) \rightarrow \sim Vx]$$

> *behavioreme*
> *biopoetic*
> *boustrophedon*
> *bees*
> *be*

---

7. I looked forward to meeting Alfrud Adlur and Sagmund Fraud.

derivative

In my dream, I was driving a car. I don't know if I was a baby, but I was driving a car, doing things with my feet, and glancing at the mirrors and holding the wheel. It was an unusual dream for me because I was actually a part of it. I was proud to be driving the car. To me, driving a car was certainly a function of genius. So, in my dream, I was genius enough to drive a car. Mo and Inflato were sitting behind me, strapped in oversized children's safety seats. They were amazed that I could drive and they kept saying so.

"How is it you can drive all of a sudden?" they asked.

"I'm a genius," I told them. And then I asked, "Why didn't you tell me that driving was so much fun?"

"It's also dangerous," my mother said.

I turned to look back at them. "And why is that?" I asked.

They both screamed. "Keep your eyes on the road!" Inflato said.

"You two are making me nervous," I said. "I'm going to stop this thing." Then I realized that I didn't know how to stop. "How do I make it stop?"

"Step on the brake pedal," Inflato said.

All of a sudden, my legs were pudgy, baby legs, and I couldn't reach any of the pedals.

"It's the one in the middle," Inflato said.

And I couldn't see through the windshield. All I could see was the bottom of the steering wheel, which was turning this way and that without my assistance. I looked back at my parents. They screamed and I screamed with them.

umstände

As Boris carried me back to the car so that we could drive to our quarters, I wrote a note:

I will need many books.

Steimmel took it and read, then said, "I'll get you all the books you want. You can have all the books and all the paper and as many different-colored pens as you like."

"I think you should be careful the way you talk to him," Boris sad.

"Are you afraid of him, Boris?"

"Frankly, Dr. Steimmel, I am."

"Don't worry, Boris. I'll protect you from the big bad baby."

excessive alliteration is a sign of an arrested imagination — or worse

Boris read the note and laughed.

Steimmel was halfway into the car. "What's so funny?"

"Nothing," Boris said. "Nothing at all."

causa sui

"Truth and falsity. Sense and nonsense. Self and nonself. Reason and madness. Centrality and marginality. The only thing standing between any of these properties is a drawn line. But a line has no depth, no depth, and so is no boundary at all. Its ends are merely positions in space and as such mean only something to each other by some orientation that might be a line, straight or curved. And so, I know I occupy some point in space *sane* because I can see and orient myself in relation to another point *insane* and as I observe the line that gives them both meaning, I realize that the line does not separate them, but connects them. And I realize as well, my heart pounding that I can, since I have two points and a line, find other points beyond the point *insane* and that I really cannot tell which point is which since points in space have no dimension. Likewise, it is true as I look behind me at the endpoint *sane* that it is really no endpoint at all. So, the line goes that way behind me and this way in front of me and I can't tell where on the line I am standing and so I bisect that line with another line and I say that *insane* is over there. But how do I know that it has not circled around behind me? How do I know that the point on the line *insane* has not planned it this way? Maybe I should walk forward so that it cannot sneak up behind me. Maybe I should run. Or maybe the point *insane* hasn't moved at all and has planned it that way. Perhaps the point *sane* has abandoned me. Maybe the two points are working together. I am not paranoid. I am not paranoid. I just won't move. That's it. I will stay right where I am, fixed in space." Emil Staiger sipped from the glass of water he clutched in sweating hands. "Do you know what I mean?"

"I know exactly what you mean," said J. Hillis Miller. "I used to have a car like that. Sometimes, when it was really cold, it would never start."

"I forgot to include real and unreal. And dead and alive. The bracketed and the unbracketed." Staiger screamed as loud as he could and hurled his glass against the far wall, breaking and streaking the flocked wallpaper.

"It was a Mercedes, that car."

"Tell me, Miller, all things considered, do you think anyone will remember who we were?"

"Hell, no."

subjective-collective

Boris pulled into a parking slot in front of cottage 3A and turned off the engine. Before Steimmel could open her door and get out, a woman had run up and given a light tap on the window. Steimmel rolled down the glass and asked, "Who are you?"

"I'm Anna Davis. We met at a symposium a couple of years ago. In Brussels. I do work with primates."

"The monkey lady," Steimmel said.

The appellation "monkey lady" did not seem to please the woman, but she went on without pause. "Yes, that's me. I didn't expect to see you here."

"Well, here I am." Steimmel pushed open the door and got out. "Boris, this is the monkey lady I told you about. Dr. Davis, I'd like you to meet my associate, Mr. Mertz."

Davis looked into the backseat at me. "So, tell me about the human infant," she said.

"Maybe later," Steimmel told her. "We're in a hurry to set up."

"The chimpanzee I'm working with has mastered American sign language." She stepped away and watched as Steimmel retrieved me from the car and Boris grabbed the bags and files. "That's an infant of African descent, isn't it? Are you studying the development of minority-status offspring?"

"Not now, Davis. Maybe later."

"Okay. Maybe we can get your baby together with my chimp."

flatus vocis

It was very much like my crib at home. Slats of wood behind which I would be placed on a soft mattress with blankets, but it was different, the slats rising higher and then joining another panel of slats on the top. It was a cage. Steimmel opened the thing up, put me in, and latched the door. She tossed a couple of books into the cage with me and proceeded to unpack her files. Boris stood staring at me behind the bars.

"Dr. Steimmel," Boris said. "I don't think we should lock the baby up like that. It's kind of like abuse."

"Is the baby starving?" Steimmel asked.

"No, doctor."

"Is the baby too hot or too cold?"

"No, doctor."

"Does the baby seem in any way uncomfortable to you?"

"No, doctor."

"Then shut up and go outside and get the rest of the equipment from the car." Steimmel came over and looked down at me. "This is your home for a while." She clicked her tongue against the roof of her mouth as she peered about the room. As I sat there observing her face, I realized that she was in fact homely, but not as homely as I had first thought. The light coming through the curtains gave her features a favorable cast.

Boris came in with a heavy box and set it on the desk. "So, what are we going to do about Davis?"

"Fuck her," Steimmel said. "I don't have time for monkey ladies. Fucking zookeepers. Piaget was a fucking zookeeper."

"She's going to come back around," Boris said. "What if she figures out that the child is kidnapped?"

"You think that ape is hers? She's here because she stole it from some-damn place." Steimmel shook her head. "That's what this place is for, Boris. If you want to keep a secret, you come here. If you want to put a pig's heart in a human being, you do it here."

"So, you think it's okay for the kid to sleep in here alone?"

"Sure. Why not?"

Boris gave Steimmel a disbelieving look. "Because he's only a year and a half old, that's why."

"You can sleep in here if you want to. It's probably a good idea. That ape woman might come snooping around. I'll call the desk and get a cot sent over." Steimmel clapped her hands and kept them together. "I'm going to shower and get some rest."

"What about Ralph?" Boris said. "He's probably hungry."

"Go to the kitchen. They must have bananas there for that chimp. Mash some up and get some milk and feed him."

bedeuten

Given the rates of phyletic evolution through the history of the Earth, it was quite possible, at least in the bugging eyes of Steimmel, that I might even represent a kind of evolutionary burst. Of course, her interest was not that, but the thought must have occurred to her as a kind of peripheral money-making possibility. She had brought along a couple of books concerning paleontology and evolution. These were the books she left with me that first night. Boris did indeed sleep on a cot in the cottage with me and he even unlatched my cage door and left the lid up. I felt, more or less, as

I did at home in my crib. I read that night about the Devonian Period and the Eocene, Oligocene, and Miocene epochs, and learned more about the evolution of the horse than anyone needs to know.

molarization
lophiodonty

To Boris:

I need some type of hard crackers.
I'm teething and I'm getting cranky.

Pronounced Articulations

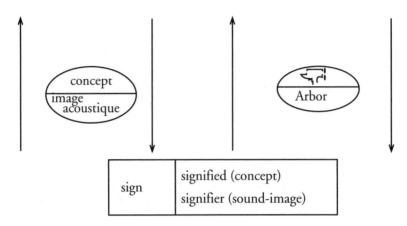

SAUSSURE

C

différance

Ecce Signum. There was an outdoor lamp that shone through the window just behind my new container. I was caged, but I could read. And I was caged, more than less, held illegally and clandestinely and against my will by someone who did not have my best interests at heart. It was certainly a screaming injustice, and had I been one for screaming, I would have. It was indeed a substantial injustice, but it was far from tragedy, in spite of the torture my parents were no doubt experiencing. I felt, in fact, privileged. Instead of spending day after endless day in the same surrounds, staring at the same walls, hearing the same voices, reading the same books, sucking the same nipples,[1] I was out in the world at large, meeting people, going places. And better, the world was a secret one. I was a prisoner and an abductee, but I was, in my way, willing.

I was more than an innocent among the advantage-taking, sin-ridden heathens in a furtive world of professionals hell-bent on advancing personal fame. I was a babe in the woods. My circumstance, however, was not so upsetting to me, one of my dispositive characteristics being a kind of buoyant patience. I was ready and eager, naiveté my fuel, to watch the events unfold. I had read that young adults often entertained notions of immortality, but such delusions paled next to my complete absence of any concept of mortality. As well, no delusion of mine was sustained by hormones, dime novels, or television. Lacking a past, and so having no

---

1. Contact with which had become decidedly more limited before my abduction, especially the case after Mo came to realize that I was not a simple-minded, milk-sucking, defecation machine.

comprehension of future, I lived for the moment as a way to make the beat generation envious. My life was but a moment. My ideas and knowledge were more-or-less present; I didn't know what waiting was, so I didn't become anxious or apprehensive. To me the endgame was no different from the opening moves.

degrees

Although I was being toted around nearly all the time, I was developing stronger leg muscles. While sitting in the car I did isometric exercise, squeezing my knees together for a few seconds at a time. In my crib, I did deep knee bends while holding onto the rails. Just standing, bouncing, and walking around the confines of my cage I felt new strength and better balance. I was quick and small and my captors were big, slow, and lacking considerable attention spans.

some early threat of promise

The first meal taken together was the following morning's breakfast. After a bit of arguing, Boris finally told Steimmel that he was taking me to the dining room whether she wanted me there or not. Go, Boris. As well, Boris made an early trip to the nearest market and bought baby food and cereal and zwieback. Boris was a good man.

The dining room was ostentatious, crowded with heavy furniture and ornate lamps, but lit mainly by a gigantic chandelier of hundreds of multicolored, faceted glass spheres tethered on a too-small-looking chain. The table was long, the dark wood visible through the lace tablecloth. Jelloffe greeted guests at the double-door entry and instructed them where to sit, but Steimmel ignored him and sat the three of us in a row, she and Boris on either side of me. I stood in the chair, my little white sneakers pressing into the cushioned seat.

Doctor Steimmel
Doctor Davis
Doctor Jelloffe
Doctor Kiernan
Doctor Kiernan

They all introduced themselves informally, smiling and pulling grapes from the platters of fruit in front of them. Standing on a chair directly opposite me was Davis's chimpanzee. I had never seen an ape and I was fascinated, the more because it was more or less my size. Well, actually the chimp was quite a bit larger, but was so much smaller than the adults that I felt some bond with him. His name was Ronald and he wouldn't keep still. Dr. Davis exhibited remarkable patience and treated the animal with much the same gentleness that I had experienced with Mo. Davis talked to Ronald with a soothing voice and fed him with her fingers, slices of banana and wedges of orange. She even let the ape drink from her own water glass.

seme

Steimmel was going to uncover the secrets of language acquistion and the mechanism of meaning by cutting open my brain. But she didn't tell anyone at the table that. She told them that I "was a mildly retarded, nonspeaking toddler with exceptional manual dexterity." She lit a cigarette and blew smoke across the table. "I'm working on motor skills." She sat there, smoking, continually smoothing out the lap of her khaki skirt, and left it at that.

Davis was going to show that apes were people too, that only the differently constructed larynxes of humans, allowing for a great range of vocal sounds, made us distinct. Her ape knew over ninety-five signs and could even construct simple sentences. Her ape could spell six five-letter words. Her ape liked some television shows and detested others. "He just loves CNN," she said. "And the weather." Davis was a nervous woman, her eyes darting from face to face at the table, though they never rested on mine. Whether she was looking for approval, I can't say, but it was clear that she was not shy about her work. She must have been comfortable with the veil of covertness that covered the resort, but still her eyes darted. "Ronald also shits in the toilet. However, we're still working on flushing." After a round of hearty and overly polite laughter, Davis looked at me as if to ask if I could do that.

Doctors Kiernan were wife and husband psychiatrists from northern Minnesota and they believed a return to the the thinking of the eighteenth century was the path to doing away with mental disorders, believing as they did that all madness, and they insisted on calling it madness, was due to the absence of reason. They wanted to *purify* bodies, awaken patients, and force the return of reason. As they spoke, taking sentences in turn, they became more animated, their eyes glowing, the husband Kiernan even appearing to drool at one point.

"We use water mostly."

"We have the pool house and we blindfold the patient and walk him around and when he least expects it, we push him in."

"The shock we hope will restore reason."

"We also use a big tub."

"A terribly large container."

"We tie a patient down and act really upset with him."

"We convince him that we're truly angry and fed up."

"Then we begin to fill the tub with water."

"We let the level rise and rise, until it's lapping at the tip of the patient's nose."

"It's a kind of baptism."

When asked if the therapy became expected after a couple of times and so ineffective, one of the Kiernans said, "That's why we've brought fifteen subjects."

"And they are raving mad, let me tell you."

"You'd be surprised how nearly drowning to death can be repeated as a startling event."

"All this brouhaha about mental disease is just a ploy to get grant money for drugs and hospitals."

"Believe me, if you take a paranoid-schizophrenic and point a .44 magnum at his forehead and pull the trigger, he'll straighten out."[2]

"One way or the other."

The Doctors Kiernan laughed.

Dr. Jelloffe said little during the meal, but listened intently, laughing at the doctors' jokes, and asking occasionally if anyone needed anything. And when someone did, he would pass the information along to one of the

---

2. What I saw as rather obvious symptoms of what the Kiernans would have called madness seemed to be lost on the others at the table. Leaving me to wonder what, in any case, irony actually signaled, doubt or certainty. And the more I looked at them, the stranger they became and likewise the more painfully, obviously bland and predictable. I imagined the two of them driving around Duluth in the middle of February, dizzied by their shared lunacy, picking up alcoholics from tavern parking lots, and dumping them into the waters of Lake Superior.

three servants who were standing close enough to hear the request anyway. He was the only one of them who smiled at me, even asked Steimmel if he could have one of his people, as he called them, "heat up a little milk for the tike."

Jelloffe did ask near the end of the meal, "Dr. Steimmel, what kinds of things does the baby write?"

"Write?" Steimmel asked.

"Yes, he wrote me a note at the desk, a very funny note. At least, he handed the note to me."

"He does make letters," Steimmel said, slowly. "A function of his superior maunual dexterity, but as far as writing notes—" She laughed and looked at Boris, nudged him with her eyes, and so he chuckled, too.

"I could have sworn," Jelloffe said.

"That would be something," Davis said, staring at me from across the table, her monkey climbing all over her. "That would be something indeed."

donne lieu

It might be said of me that I am a throwback to the Renaissance, not insofar as I am particularly accomplished in several areas or even one, but because I create not as an act of expression, but rather to exercise my craft, whether poetic or not. This in spite of my autobiographical pretensions and my rather bold assumption that my observations and analyses will be of interest to anyone else. But neither is it quite true that I consider my art an objective discipline, which by the imitation and practice of rhetorical devices is made better or more beautiful.

> *Weialala leia*
> *Wallala leialala*

What I did do in my little crib with pen and paper was not a turnpike to personal freedom. Nor did I engage in the description or illustration of societal or cultural truths. I was, after all, a baby, a baby being held captive. Social truths could have no meaning for me. Morality was a mere vapor, a unicorn of a notion. National character was a distant target with no identifying attributes. I was indeed an island. Baby Island. But even then I did not disavow a social role for myself as artist, but simply found the designation unintelligible. I felt no guilt for this. I felt no guilt about anything. I understood, abstractly, the concept of guilt, could spot it in stories and novels without explicit notification of the condition, but I did not have the proper *stuff* to experience it. Even if I had, I would not have fallen for it. Baby Island. Fuck them all.[3]

> *Don Quixote, thus unhappily hurt, was extremely sullen and melancholy.*

Apathy, as I saw it, had a bad reputation, being seen as the wall at the end of a dead-end alley. But in that alley, at the very wall itself, I found necessary possibility. It was irony incarnate, a condition that required, at least, the energy to turn away, more energy than is required in a crisis to act heroic. For apathy took thought, decision. Not caring was no mean feat. While engaged in apathetic meditation, options appeared clearly, much like projected images on a screen, two-dimensional and harmless, but present nonetheless. Apathy was not a head buried in the sand, but a position taken on high ground. (Perhaps even next to the artillery.)[4]

ephexis

> *Copora Cavernosa*

> *Body of*
> *and body without,*
> *curved against itself,*
> *consisting of two fibrous,*
> *cylindrical tubes,*
> *side by side.*

---

3. *From Thomas Moore's "The Fire-Worshippers":*
   Oh! ever thus from childhood's hour,
      I've seen my fondest hopes decay;
   I never lov'd a tree or flower,
      But 'twas the first to fade away.
   I never nurs'd a dear gazelle,
      To glad me with its soft black eye,
   But when it came to know me well,
      And love me, it was sure to die!

4. To say, "I do not care" requires an effort that truly being without concern would not generate. If John does not care that you have scratched his new car with your rusty nail, then he will drive away without a word. My apathy is to your apathy what our present notion of atheism is to the fifteenth and sixteenth centuries' notion of atheism.

It is connected,
intimately,
along the median line,
in a filamentous envelope,
longitudinal, circular

like the movements
which cause the changes,
the internal threads filling,
strings elastic.

Fibers,
fibrils,
elongated cells,
bands, chords,
trabeculae,
muscle,
arteries,
nerves,
fibers.

incision

Steimmel stood at the window and of the laboratory (Ralph's room) and held back the curtain for a furtive peek outside. She sucked on her cigarette and said to Boris without looking at him, "Did you see the way she was looking at the kid? I tell you, that monkey lady is up to no good."

les fous avaient alors une vie facilement errante

"What harm can she do? You said yourself that she's here with a stolen ape." Boris put another couple of books in the cage with me, gave me a brief smile. "If you ask me, everybody in this place is certifiable."

la folie est déjà en porte-à-faux à l'intérieur de ce monde de la déraison

"We'll have to put up with them. What I'm worried about is the Kiernan subjects getting loose and running amuck." She dropped her butt on the floor and stepped on it with toe of her espadrille. "I really hate that monkey lady. I remember her from Brussels pretty vividly now. She gave a paper on the functions of animal semiosis or some shit. She's got more than monkeys on her mind. She's interested in language. I bet she would like to get our Ralph together with—what's that monkey's name?"

dans les maisons d'interement

"Ronald."

la folie voisine avec toutes les formes de la déraison

"Ronald? What kind of name is that for an ape? Bobo or Cheetah or Kong, now those are ape names. Ronald, my ass."[5]

$$(x)(Cx \rightarrow \sim Vx) \vdash (x)[(Cx\&Px) \rightarrow \sim Vx]$$

Steimmel again subjected me to the same simple-minded puzzles she had put before me the first time. I put blocks into holes and just to amuse her, I put a square peg into a round hole. We played the memory game and I wrote out for her a string of two hundred thirty-five rapidly spoken words, phrases, and equations.

But still I could not completely control my waste functions. Boris did set me on the toilet periodically, but he would wait at the door instead of leaving me alone. Perhaps he thought I would fall in and drown. At any rate, probably indulgently, I blamed him for my slow progress. Finally, I did

---

5. I wondered what would make a good name for a monkey. Especially since Steimmel did not even know the monkey. And so I wondered about my name and then names in general. I understood that my name was Ralph and that Ralph was my name and that there other people out in the world, dead and alive, who also answered to Ralph. Was it the case that my name *Ralph* was not the name of Mr. Bunch or Mr. Nader, but my own special *Ralph,* just as the *ball* of tennis was not the *ball* of Cinderella? Was the *Ralph* that all three of us shared a kind of ideal *Ralph,* Ralphness perhaps, a kind of denotation while my private *Ralph* was just a connotative manifestion of *Ralph?* Certainly by naming me Ralph, my parents had done something very significant. They had indeed *named* me, but what else had been done to me by my having been *named* Ralph? What did it mean for me to be Ralph, or a Ralph, or a Ralph against my will or by choice? Was I necessarily *Ralph* or only contingently *Ralph?* Would I have been me had my parents named me Kong or Bobo? And I suppose that if I changed my name to Bobo that upon finding me years later, my parents would say, "Yes, it is Ralph. See, there's the birthmark on his tush." And after I made it known to them that my name was Bobo, they would say, "Oh, no. You're Ralph, all right. We'd know you anywhere."

what I should have done in the first place, which was to write him a note asking for a little privacy. He complied and with a copy of *The Morphology of Meaning for Retarded Children* on my lap, I learned to do my do.

But back to Steimmel. She subjected me to the Kaufman Assessment Battery, measured me by the McCarthy scales of children's abilities, the Wechsler scale of intelligence, the Stanford-Binet scale, testing my pictorial memory, my fluency, my ability to draw analogies, my ability to wind through mazes, my concept of geometric design, and in every case I scored either off the charts or as a complete moron. Steimmel, like my parents, was irritated by my refusal to speak. She examined my throat and checked my reflexes with her little hammer. She tried to startle me, hoping to cause me to blurt out something, but I didn't. I was only immediately amused that her treatment was not so unlike that of the Kiernans. She pinched me, trying to make me cry out, but only left a silent bruise, which Boris yelled at her about. She tried to measure how quickly I read and how much I was capable of understanding. She tried to engage me in conversation, but was finally too impatient to await my written responses. She was convinced that I was terribly strange, terribly bright, out of control, a freak of nature, and she had no idea how it was I knew how to use language. Her chain-smoking got worse. She took to drink. She either slept all day or not at all. She asked me if I knew the devil. She asked me if I had ever seen god. She asked me if there was a god. She asked what I hoped to achieve by doing so many knee bends while she spoke to me. She told me she was lucky to have found me, that I was lucky she had found me, that she hated me, that she would lock me in a room with Ronald the chimp if I didn't cooperate.

"What's the first word you remember?" she asked. She had me lying on a little sofa while she sat beside me, her legs crossed, a cigarette dangling from the tips of her fingers.

I don't recall.

"Did your parents talk to you a lot when you were first born?"

Not really. They talked to each other.

"Did you resent that?"

No.

"What would you call your first word?"

I don't understand the question.

Steimmel looked away and out the window. "There must be something you remember hearing. Even if it wasn't the first word. What was the first word you can remember making an impression on you?"

I don't recall.

"Think!"

I thought. I thought to say milk or nipple just to pacify her, but either would have been false.

Iconicity.

"You're pulling my fucking leg."

Signification?

She stared at me and blew a smoke ring.

Paralanguage?

"Boris!" she called out.

Proxemics

Boris appeared in the doorway.
"Take this . . . this thing back to his *crib*."

unties of simulacrum

> *conceptio*
> *confirmatio*
> *connotatio*
> *codex vivus*

ARISTOPHANES: All war is unnecessary and finally ruinous for all parties, but yet I find that the notion of sincere reconciliation doesn't appear as an option for humans, or for politicians either.

ELLISON: Perhaps. But the condition you call war is often the condition of life for many. We have in our time a musician who clowns before kings and queens, wipes down his sweating brow with a rag between creating the sweetest music with the same lips and breath that make a graveled growl of a voice. He is at war. Necessarily and perhaps forever. And his weapon is irony. The enemy loves what he does, but when they imitate him, try to make it themselves, they hate him because, not only do they fail to recreate his music, but they are terrified of becoming the one they mimic.

ARISTOPHANES: But why would anyone even be afraid of becoming the one who makes such fine music as you describe?

ELLISON: The surface answer is because of the color of his skin.

ARISTOPHANES: The color of his skin? I do not understand your time. Was he an odd color that spread like disease to those around him?

ELLISON: No. Finally, I think it must be because of the power of his art. His music, what we hope for words, strips away the illusory veil covering our culture, and leaves the world a painfully clear reality. The practice is beautiful, the vision often is not.

ARISTOPHANES: Back to his color. Is he a color other people are not?

ELLISON: No, there are many people who share his color and they are hated, too. But it has nothing to do with color. Don't you see? The color is an excuse. It could be his god or his smell or his ideas. It could even be that he is an infant. Finally, it's because living, for him and people like him, has become an art, just waking up and getting out of bed is an act of creation. This scares all the people of my time, even the ones who make the art.

ARISTOPHANES: Art has always scared people. Art always will. And it will always scare those of us who make it the most. I suppose I know why. Our intelligence, our reason, our dialectic comes, perhaps, from the gods, but art, art comes from us without doubt. The artist is self-elected and so there is no pity, no excuse, only blame. And, of course, people are more afraid of infants than anything else.

ELLISON: Of course, that's true.

bridge

Everyone knew that I was the kidnapped baby from Los Angeles, but as Steimmel had pointed out to Boris, their crimes, though perhaps not as grave, were serious enough, and none of them had any interest in turning in Steimmel. Least of all, Jelloffe. His business hinged on complete confidentiality and his crimes, cumulatively, were no doubt the greatest. What he had condoned and so conveniently overlooked made him at least an accomplice after the fact.

Steimmel was becoming more nervous and crazier by the day, not because she feared what I have already stated was so unlikely, namely being given up to the police, but because she didn't know how to proceed with her dissection of me. My answers to her questions, though frequently truthful, were proving unhelpful, and so she resorted to performing the same tests on me, once more, over and over again with results so varied that she even once broke down and fell to her knees crying. Boris and I watched her descent together and, as my reading had suggested, such mutual witnessing caused us to become close. Perhaps not quite friends, but more like two sailors, one from the galley and the other from the engine room, awaiting rescue while clinging to the same floating deck chair.

ens realissimum

It was not a few times that I saw the face of Davis pressed up against the window of my room. I don't how much she was able to see or how much she could have inferred if she had seen everything. She saw me doing my exercises and she saw me reading through one or another of the many books Boris had been bringing me from the institute's rather nicely endowed library, but for all I knew she was aware only of my ability to turn a page. Perhaps, finally, that's all I really did, having assumed that condition which was far too familiar, intense boredom. At least, at home I was sometimes amused by Inflato's posturing and lack of self-consciousness about it, but Steimmel was the same, same, same every day, every hour. I hesistated to call her predictable, because that would have implied the possibility of something different. She was like gravity or the second law of thermodynamics. So, Davis's face, and her ape's, were actually somewhat welcomed. Finally, when it was clear that I was in the room alone or that Boris was sound asleep on his cot, Davis would tap on the panes and wave to me. And she would have Ronald wave, too. I just stared at them, realizing that perhaps the muscles of my baby face didn't allow the range of expression I would have liked.

exousai

Boris sat at the desk, either making notes or playing crosses and naughts with himself. He was bored, the symptoms were unmistakable: listless sighing, absent scratching at the back of the head, overstated widening of the eyes as if to keep them open. It had been two weeks since our arrival and, though the communal meals had proven wooden, tedious, vapid, and stultifying, I, and apparently Boris as well, missed them, since Steimmel had decided that we shouldn't attend because it was likely someone might figure out my real secret. Boris might even have been asleep and his hand working without him at the desk, because when a knock sounded at the door he nearly popped from his skin, then looked at the pencil in his hand as if to wonder what it was doing there. The knock came again. Boris went to the door and listened.

"Dr. Steimmel?" he said, softly.

"No, it's me, Dr. Davis."

Boris looked over at me and then put his ear back to the door. "Dr. Steimmel isn't here."

"I came to see you."

Boris cleared his throat and grimaced. "Dr. Steimmel isn't here and you really should go away."

"Come on, let me in," Davis said. "I've brought you a little something. And something for the little boy as well."

Boris looked again at me, then wiped his hands on his trousers. "I'm going to open the door, but I'm telling you, you've got to get out of here before Dr. Steimmel gets back." He opened the door and stood in the middle of the opening.

"Did I wake you?"

"Oh, no." Boris smoothed his hair back with a hand. "I was just sitting and thinking." He looked down and stared at Ronald. Davis was holding the chimp's hand. "Hi, Ronald."

"Wave to Boris, Ronald."

Ronald was as subdued as I had ever seen him, but he did wave, then nonchalantly took in the rest of the room.

"Well, aren't you going to let us in?" Davis asked.

"No."

"Come on, Boris. You know, I'm all right. Besides, how can I give you your surprise if you don't let me in?"

"Well, okay. But really, make it quick. If Steimmel finds you here, she'll kill me, or worse."

"What could be worse than death?" Davis asked.

Boris just laughed.

"Where is Dr. Steimmel?" She was in the room now, her eyes darting the way they did.

"I don't know. Asleep, maybe. She hasn't been in all day. She's depressed." Then Boris shut up as if he'd said too much.

"She's kind of nervous."

Boris nodded, staring at Davis.

"Oh, your surprise," she said. She dug down into her large straw bag and came up with a small, wrapped box. "It's not much, but I thought you'd like it." She handed it to him.

Boris was visibly moved, perhaps his hands were even shaking a little. "It's even wrapped. Thank you."

"Go ahead, open it."

Boris opened the box and though I strained my baby eyes there at the rail of my cage, I could not see what it was, but whatever it was made Boris blush. He squeezed out an awkward smile and didn't quite look at Davis directly. "I don't know what to say."

"Do you like it?"

"I love it."[6] Boris closed the box and put the thing into his pocket. "You really shouldn't have." He smiled, directly at her this time. "You said you had something for Ralph."

"Yes." Back into her bag and she produced a banana, its yellow skin now nearly all brown. "I thought the little fellow might like some fresh fruit. Since you haven't been in to meals lately."

"Well, we've got plenty of food in here, but thanks. Ralph loves bananas." Boris flashed a nervous glance my way. His expression moved to-

---

6. "Suppose everyone had a box with something in it: we call it a 'beetle.' No one can look into anyone else's box, and everyone says he knows what a beetle is only by looking at *his* beetle—Here it would be quite possible for everyone to have something different in his box. One might even imagine such a thing constantly changing—But suppose the word 'beetle' had a use in people's language?—If so, it would not be used as the name of that thing. The thing in the box has no place in the language game at all; not even as a *something:* for the box might be empty—No, one can 'divide through' by the thing in the box; it cancels out, whatever it is." (Wittgenstein's *Philosophical Investigations,* no. 293) I pondered this as I stood on the designation that was my mattress, but realized that the object of that designation was irrelevant, and that mattress was not even the name of that thing. But what did I know of grammatical rules and language games, my having come to language without actually learning it? It was there in front of me and the thing I called language was not a thing at all, except when Steimmel wanted to know how it worked or when Ronald the ape tried to sign a covert message to me. I was in fact the beetle in the box.

"Why about you!" Tweedledee exclaimed, clapping his hands together triumphantly. "And if he left off dreaming about you, where do you suppose you'd be?"

ward panic as he saw me scribbling on my pad. "You'll have to go now," he said, trying to turn Davis around.

But the woman let go of the chimpanzee's hand and the animal took off across the room. "Ronald, you come back here," she said. "You come back here right now. I'm sorry"

"Well, just get him fast."

Davis walked toward the ape, not looking at him but at everything else. "Come on, Ronald." Ronald signed something at her. "Not funny, Ronald. Now be a good chimp and let's go back to our cottage."

Ronald dragged his knuckles toward my cage. I must admit that I found his size and evident strength somewhat intimidating. Still, though, I learned much as I observed the way the animal used leverage to move his body about. Ronald slammed shut the top of my cage and I fell to my butt on the mattress.

"Hey, that's a cage," Davis said.

"Not really," Boris said. "Well, it is, but it isn't. We couldn't find a crib." Davis was next to me now, looking all around me, but not so much at me. Boris was pulling her arm. "I think I hear Dr. Steimmel coming."

"What's this?" Davis asked, picking up my notepad.

"Some of Dr. Steimmel's notes," Boris said.

"I don't think so," Davis said. "This note says, 'Boris, I like bananas as much as you like Steimmel.' Did he write that?"

"Of course not."

"Boris, he had to write it." She stepped back and stared at me. "Oh, my god. Oh, my god."

spacing

Hit cin rinny, rainy woony for jest su lung
end din ye laugh tew sewim.
Eat does ant reely mater ow! fest hit flews,
eeks wair zey pit ye end.

libidinal economy

Steimmel was large by my estimation, hardly a giant, but her feet sounded as if they weighed hundreds of pounds each as we all heard her approach along the wooden walk.

"Oh, my god!" Davis said, but for a different reason, still staring at me.

"Hide!" Boris shouted in a whisper. "Hide someplace."

Even Ronald seemed to appreciate the gravity of the situation, his monkey feet pitty-patting in place while his mother tried to figure out what they were going to do.

"Under the crib," Boris said. "And pull this blanket over you."

"Okay," Davis said.

Thud. Thud. Thud. The footsteps drew nearer.

"And Boris?"

"What?"

Davis kissed Boris on the lips. I watched the man's eyes glaze over. Then he found himself and said, "Now, get under there and be quiet. Please, be quiet."

umstände

The next step is more complex. It requires skinning the mules or the goats and making the shell of a balloon, which is then filled with hot air and raised to an altitude of some three hundred feet having tethered to it a basket constructed of bones and reeds and straw and chicken feathers and when it's as high as it's supposed to be, one shoots at it with a slingshot, trying not to bring it down, but to scare it higher. But who is in the basket to be frightened higher? It is Nobody. Nobody went up in it, there is Nobody in it to be scared, and it will come down with Nobody still in it. And Nobody will go up unless one of us does, however, of course, if I go up alone and someone asks you who is in the basket with me . . .

tubes 1 … 6

The Dura Mater

Dense and inelastic,
fibrous,
lining the inner wall
of my skull,
thick where the headaches
live.

The outer surface
is uneven, fibrillated,
clinging
to the inner veneer,
opposite sutures

there at the base,
the smooth insides.
Four processes
press inward,
into the cavity,

supporting, protecting,
prolonged to the outer skin
where the irrevocable
dreams evaporate.

peccatum originale

"What in the world of psychoanalytic shit is going on in here?" Steimmel asked. She was, I believe, intoxicated. Her swaying and the way she held the empty bottle by its neck suggested it. She looked around the room suspiciously. "I know you, Boris. I know you like a book and something is up." She stared at him. "You're shaking. Talk, you little beetle!"

"I don't know what you're talking about."

Steimmel looked over at me. "Of course you don't. And neither does our pint-sized lexicon over here." She walked toward me. "I'm going to figure out how you work. Even if I have to literally cut open your head and peek into your brain. Little smart ass. I hate you."

"Dr. Steimmel, you're drunk," Boris said, and none too assertively.

"Oh, you determined this on your own? That's why you're the great scientist you are, Boring-is." She turned her back to me and started back toward Boris. "Your acute powers of observation. Tell me, what hidden clue tipped you off to my condition?"

"Please, Dr. Steimmel."

"Boris, when I'm done with the little bastard, I'm going to take it upon myself to give you a spine. How does that sound?"

Beneath my crib, Ronald must have moved, because Davis whispered, "Shut up."

"What did you say?" Steimmel said, turning back to me. Then she stopped. "You said something. Did you hear him, Boris?"

"No, Dr. Steimmel."

"Well, I did. I heard him as plain as day. As plain as the nose on your face. As plain as that Davis-monkey-woman-doctor." Steimmel laughed and approached me. "Say something else, tiny wonder."

You're mistaken. I said nothing.

She read the note, none too easily, holding it this distance and that, attempting to focus. Behind her, Boris looked about, ready to bolt. I could see that my note was of concern to him.

"You did, too," Steimmel snapped at me. "You've been holding back." Something inside her made a sudden attack and she fought to swallow. "Boris," she said, "I'm going to my cottage to be sick. When I get back, be ready to get to work." Then she staggered out.

Boris closed the door, locked it, and leaned against it. "You can come out," he said.

Davis and Ronald reappeared. "She's a lunatic," Davis said.

Ronald was signing like crazy, but nobody was looking at him.

"I've gone along with this for too long," Boris said. "I've got to get this child back to his parents."

"Let's calm down a little bit here," Davis said.

"Are you kidding? Dr. Steimmel might just cut open that baby's head. She's that crazy."

"Okay, okay, okay. I'll help you. Tonight, you meet me in the parking lot with the kid. I'll go pack up. All right?" Davis was bobbing and weaving, trying to catch Boris's eyes.

"I don't know, Dr. Davis."

Davis stepped close to Boris and planted another kiss on his lips. "You know, darling."

I thought Boris would faint. "I'll be there."

"At nine."

Boris nodded.

ennuyeux

I wanted to know things, though I was at a loss to say why. Perhaps because boredom was a constantly threatening, lurking enemy, though when it caught me, and it often did, it was hardly as fascinating an attack as might have come from a different enemy. It was boring. I tried to find the malevolence, the brutality, even the malignancy of it a curiosity, something at least to measure, but it was only and simply boring. And so, the enemy was the worse enemy, not even threatening harm, only attack. The anxiety produced by my anticipation of its onset was dreadful, and so the two accompanying enemies, anticipation and anxiety, were in their way worse, for they were present at all times the boredom was not. Books helped, but I was so voracious and ravenous a reader that I was hard-pressed to stay ahead of the beast. On occasion I would latch onto an idea that was all consuming, but the anxiety that the absorption would pass detracted from the full pleasure of the experience. Finally, I was a sad baby, frequently amused, often pleasantly puzzled, and intensely arrested by subjects, but sad, beaten-down by my own demons.

My mother was driven by a fear that there was something in her to be expressed that might not get out. She was not so much afraid that the thing yet to be expressed would fester and corrode within her if it remained. She was afraid she would be cheating herself, as well as that thing, that she would be cheating me by teaching me by example that there was nothing beyond the material world. Mo was noble in that way.

My father, on the other hand, though not without talent, and in spite of my ridicule, not without intellect, was afraid of not appearing as a figure on the *cutting edge*. Ideas were only marginally of interest, his primary need being community. And for whatever reason, he needed to be an elected official of that community, whether mayor or dog catcher. He claimed loyalty to the working class, but hated his roots so much that he could hardly conceal his disdain for blue-collar tastes and the manifestations of its values. He feared that he was to the intelligensia what a successful fast-food-franchise owner was to "old" money. He was sick with this, the disease being insidious and pernicious, and it was worse than my boredom because it was so absorbed with outward appearances.

subjective-collective

Eve sat in front of a small canvas. She did not like working small. She felt confined, contained. She wanted to cry and so held her hands in tight fists on her thighs. She refused to cry, refused to leave the work alone. She picked up a large brush and covered the panel with ebony black, laid it thick and with abandon, then just sat there looking at it. There was no expression at all, save for her anger at not being able to create anything on that surface. She laughed. She considered covering all the canvases with black, obliterating everything because of her weakness, because of her lack of talent.

Douglas walked into the studio. "What do you say we go out and find some dinner?" he asked. He went and stood behind her, observed the canvas. "Hey, you're up to something here, aren't you?"

ootheca

It goes without saying.

vita nova

Steimmel must have returned to her room and fallen asleep or passed out or slipped and hit her self-perceived oversized head on a counter, because she never returned that afternoon. Boris pulled together his things and the few articles of clothing he and Steimmel had bought for me and several books to keep me busy. He then carried me out to the parking lot where we waited in the shadows. It was raining and we were being soaked.

Then across the way, dressed in a trench coat was Davis, looking like La Berma. The monkey was at her side and they were both looking this way and that, no doubt for us. Boris whistled to them, but the rain swallowed his noise. He looked back in the direction of Steimmel's cottage and blew out a troubled breath. He put me down next to a piece of ornate statuary and told me wait there.

But I didn't wait. I did what toddlers do, what I had been waiting to do. I walked away. I walked toward the lights of cottages that were not mine or Steimmel's. My legs were strong and I was quick and before they knew it, I was out of sight, slipping along a wet gravel path and then onto a deck and through an ajar, banging-in-the-wind gate. I was too short to open any doors and too short to see through any windows. I sat under the awning of a doorway and tried to get dry. I could hear Boris and Davis calling out to me, trying not to be heard by anyone else. I wondered if apes had keen noses like dogs I had read about.

derivative

It was and is said of Byron that he was a genius, this in spite of shabby and substandard verse steeped in obvious sentiment and often garish, pretentious, and tawdry. I was a baby, as were you all, and even I not only saw through the transparent attempt at artificial elevation of self and experience, but also the insipid and childish need (I was an expert) for attention. There was no struggle for Byron, once finally free of his torturing mother and nestled within the walls of Newstead, save for the grinding self-pity over his limp and his self-knowledge of his intellectual limitations.[7] Byron would have had me believe in his time that he was ferocious, but his timidity was not so well hidden. He was not so much a cerebral storm in love with elemental sin as he was as pathetic and artless as Rousseau in his quest for simple virtue. Genius, I assume, does not recognize itself, having better things to do. At an age when parents are so quick to attribute genius to any number of pathetically simple accomplishments, I knew that I was no genius. I knew that mere acceleration held in it no truly remarkable merit. I had a headstart, only that, and like any headstart, it would be negated in the middle or at the end. What genius, I guessed then and know now, allows is the start of a new race. Genius means finding a way back to the beginning where the truths are uncorrupted and honest and maybe even pure.

mary mallon

The downpour diminished to a drizzle and I could hear the movements and voices of Boris and Davis more clearly. There was fear, genuine fear in Boris's voice and for a second I considered that he might actually be concerned about my welfare. I didn't know where I was going, but it was not back to the dissection table. And that's what Davis had in mind for me. She had seduced Boris, but not me. In fact, she hadn't even attempted to win me over, but had treated me like the object I no doubt was. I kept ahead of their voices and found myself again in the shadows of the parking lot. I walked through the lot toward the circular drive in front of the main lodge. Then a dark sedan came to a sliding, gravel-throwing stop beside me. The headlights must have been off because I had not seen it approach. When the doors opened the interior lights blinded me, but I heard men's voices.

"Just grab him and let's go," one said.

And indeed I was grabbed and hoisted into the air and into the car.

---

7. But perhaps Byron was great, like Napoleon (of his time and one of his idols), like Christ (like Byron, the Satanist, great by repetition of claim, or at least by privilege of birth), like Hitler (made so by violence and the stupidity of masses), but none were geniuses.

"How do we know he's the right kid?"

"He's the right kid."

Vexierbild

My world, for all my stealth and quick movements, was getting smaller and I could see no light at the end of the funnel. The familar movement of the car upset my stomach as I was loose in the backseat and the discomfort was aggravated by whatever colognes the two men were mingling with their body odor and the smoke of their cigar and cigarette. All I could really see of their faces was behind the hot points of their smoking.

I threw up. *Brutum fulmen.*

"Hey, he heaved all over the seat," the passenger-seat man said.

"Don't worry about it," said the driver.

"It stinks."

How could he know?

Figures and a Pair of Graphs

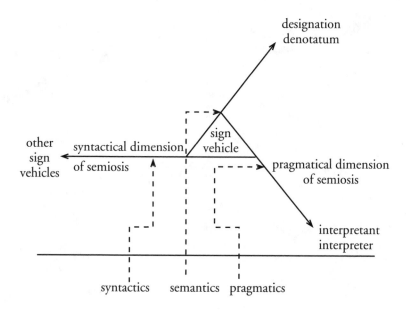

MORRIS

D

différance

From morn to noon, from noon to dewy eve, I was carried by my parents from here to there and back, was tossed into the air, had heads rubbed into my belly while suspended above the ground, was handed to strangers on whose shoulders, if I could, I would spit up my mother's nourishing but only adequate milk, and suffer through mindless compliments from mindless onlookers and my mindless parents. I had no legs, but I moved about, not because of a defiance of gravity, but because of a sickening, malignant, imposed, and necessary dependancy. And it all sat on me like a weight, a kind of self-referential density, as it was the case that whenever I was in the room, I was the object of attention, if not discussion. I was like a loaded gun resting on a table in front of a bludgeon of convicts. And like that gun, the fear seemed present in all the faces near me that I might at any second go off, whatever *going off* might come to. And so, right and wrong, truth and falsity, and clarity and confusion were not operative criteria for me. Escape was all I could think of, even if it was escape from observation for just a second or two, a bit of privacy when I could screw up my face and load my diaper, a moment to have gas without someone commenting on my smiling. I talked inwardly to myself, not separating myself into two parts at any time, but my thinking came to me as a flutist's melodies to his own ears, but the melodies were a component of me, inextricably bound to me, in no way separate or different or distant from me. My language, my thinking, was all I had, all I could have, my only deliverance and distraction and finally, my sustenance. Still, I drooled and aimed my pee at the ceiling when my diaper was peeled away.

umstände

"Douglas, why doesn't the baby make any sounds? I mean he doesn't even cry." Eve was arranging some cosmos and poppies she had picked in a vase on the table by the window.

"Count our blessings. Imagine a baby keeping us up all night long with wailing." Douglas let his book come to rest on his lap, reached to the coffee table, and grabbed a cigarette.

"But no sound at all?"

Douglas shrugged, lighting up.

"My mother said I was a quiet baby."

"Well, there you have it."

"But not this quiet."

"I'm sure there's nothing wrong, but why don't you ask the pediatrician, just to be certain."

"I did." Eve plopped down on the sofa and stared out the window. "Actually, I don't think she quite believed me." She looked over at me, wrapped up in blankets in my bassinet. "Ralph was with me and, of course, he didn't make a sound, but it doesn't seem strange for just five minutes. I told her he never cries."

"And what did she say?"

"She said, 'Count your blessings.'"

"Well, there you have it."

$(x)(Cx \rightarrow \sim Vx) \vdash (x)[(Cx \& Px) \rightarrow \sim Vx]$

The car sped like a bullet through the night. Young Ralph sat in the backseat of the modestly appointed sedan and stared forward at the goons who had nabbed him. The thugs weren't from the mob; they weren't dressed well enough. But neither were they poorly enough dressed to be cops, though they stank. And they knew enough to keep the headlights off in the parking lot, so they definitely were not cops, not regular cops anyway. Maybe they were feds. Ralph leaned against the door as the driver took a curve hard on the wet highway.

"That wasn't too tough," the shotgun rider said.

"Piece of cake," said the driver. "Hey, reach down there and gimme one of them doughnuts."

"What's the story with this kid anyway?"

"Don't know, don't care. I just drive the bus."

96

Shotgun looked into the backseat. "He don't look special."

"Something special about him." The driver finished his doughnut and licked his fingers. "What do you say we head over to that dance place, Exotica, I think it's called, after we drop off the cargo?"

"Sounds good to me. I hear they got a great Diana Ross impersonator there."

"Cher and Liza Minelli, too."

"Cool."

Vexierbild

The Other to which we turn for our identity is constipated. For Lacan, this Other is not being, but the place of speech where the assembly of the system of signifiers rests, i.e., language. Therefore the constipation of the Other is necessarily symbolic and resides in the fact that a particular signifier is in need of the Other. The missing or obscured signifier is the feces and the fact that it is missing from the Other means we cannot locate it in ourselves by appeal to the Other. Finally, the Other cannot constitute identity for us. Stated another way, "in the signifier there is nothing that guarantees the dimension of truth founded by the signifier," and, as articulating beings, our constipation lies precisely in the deficiency of a secured truth or meaning. Truth is without hope, "a truth without truth," and the Other's constipation unveils the truth that constipation is the irresistible and inevitable state of the human condition.[1]

degrees

I could still see Ronald signing like crazy in the lab after Steimmel's departure. The chimp was talking, not merely using symbols in a way that suggested some purely fixed correlation between signs and objects. I thought the ape was asking what was going on.

---

1. Constructing the tautology that says one begins at the beginning depends on the ability of both mind and language to reverse themselves, and thus to move from present to past and back again, from a complex situation to an anterior simplicity and back again, or from one point to another as if in a circle. Said, *Invention and Method*, pp. 29–30.

incision

Labyrinth

Hollowed cavities of bone,
the labyrinth contains
the clear liquor Cotunnii,
the twisting trail within.

Complex maze,
one puzzle embracing another,
the sound contained in petrous bone,
read

through membranous
contortions,
tracing through matter,
misgivings,
remembered hurts.

Semicircular canals
mock incompleteness,
returning the sound
to the medium
without.

ootheca

The room was like waiting rooms I had seen, at the doctor's office, at several other places I had gone to with my parents. I was left sitting on a deep red sofa that was placed between two matching chairs. I was alone there, the lights bright, and the buzzing of them the only sound. Occasionally, off in some other room a telephone rang.

A woman, thicker than my mother and dressed, well, motherly, came into the room all smiles and cooing sounds and she approached me directly. "So, you're little Ralph," she said. "My, my, my." She hoisted me into the air and looked into my face. "You're a handsome fellow, aren't you?" She then pulled me close and held me to her chest, my chin on her shoulder. It was not an altogether bad feeling, being held by someone more like my mother than any of the handlers I had recently experienced. She carried me from that cliché of a waiting room into a cliché of an institutional hallway. The corridor looked and felt much like the hospital in which I first met Steimmel. But from that hall, we entered what some idiot someplace considered a prime example of a child's bedroom.

There were yellow ducks swimming across the robin's egg blue walls at the join to the ceiling. There was a white crib in the middle of the room just like the one I'd slept in at home. There was a low rocking chair beside the crib with a flowered cushion tied to its seat and a multicolored braided rug on the floor in front of it. There were paintings of clowns on the walls along with photographs of hot-air balloons in blue skies, and a pile of colorful balls of varied sizes in a corner by the window. The window however was barred.

The woman put me down in the crib and I was face to face with something I had never had, but only read about, a teddy bear. The thing was half my size with fur that floated in the air, button eyes and nose, expressionless, still, and cold. She grabbed the thing and rubbed it into my belly.

"I'm Nanna," she said. "I'll be taking care of you. If you need anything, just call out for Nanna. Let me hear you say it. Come on. Nan-na."

I, of course, said nothing.

"Well, anyway, you'll be more relaxed in time. You'll find out that Nanna is here for you and that you can trust her." She looked about the room, then walked over to a bureau, opened a drawer, and pulled out a set of pajamas. She came back to me. "Nanna will put these on you and I'll give you your bath in the morning. You need a good night's sleep." She undressed me. "Would the little man like to try the potty before bed?" Her words and the sound of her voice were mesmerizing. She took my tiny naked body to the bathroom and sat me on a child's training seat atop the toilet. I did my business and she praised me as if I were a dog.

She dressed me for sleep, switched off the light, and paused at the door before closing it. "Good night, little man," she said.

seme

SOCRATES: Tell me, Jimmy, how do things go these days?

BALDWIN: Things go fine.

SOCRATES: You know, I envy you your art. Being able to create a world, build people, lie the way you do so convincingly.

BALDWIN: I wouldn't call it lying.

SOCRATES: Very well. But I have a question for you. You create a world and to do that you have to draw on the world we know and then re-create. Is that close to correct?

BALDWIN: More or less.

SOCRATES: So, in order to render a world as you do, you must fully comprehend the world from which you draw your material and substance.

BALDWIN: Actually, it is the act of creating the world of my fiction that allows me to understand the so-called real world.

SOCRATES: But how can that be when the real world is the one you need before you can begin your art? Suppose a man wanted to write a novel, but he knew nothing of the world. Could he do it?

BALDWIN: Why would such a man seek to write a novel?

SOCRATES: Just suppose he did.

BALDWIN: I can't suppose that.

SOCRATES: Let's try it this way. Suppose I understand the world completely. By virtue of that fact, would I necessarily be able to write a novel?

BALDWIN: Why would you want to?

SOCRATES: But suppose I did want to.

BALDWIN: Then you'd have no need for writing a novel.

SOCRATES: Suppose, I didn't need to, but just wanted to write a novel.

BALDWIN: Then you wouldn't understand the world.

supernumber

Nanna, or Madam Nanna, as I liked to call her in my head, came every morning, dressed in her nurse's uniform, and talked soothingly to me, fed me, sat me on the potty, threw the light-as-air inflated balls at me, and held me in her lap and rocked me while she read me stories. Stupid stories. Stories about simple-minded children and bears that talked, with improbable situations for no reason except that they were improbable. I hated them. They bored me to sleep every time. All she had to do was open one of the garishly colored, skinny volumes and I was out. A week went by and I was numbed into a weakened state. I had been keeping my talents to myself, not knowing who Madam Nanna was or what she wanted. All I knew was that she was connected with Fric and Frac, the two hoodlums who had spirited me away from the institute that rainy night.

Finally, fed up with her niceness, reeling from two pages of some story about a pig who opened a bank, I snatched the pen from the breast pocket of her uniform and wrote, beneath a picture of the pig signing a loan agreement,

Who the fuck are you?

If my message scared or even surprised her, Madam Nanna didn't let on. She just smiled sweetly at me and said, "We mustn't use such language."

She was not frightened by me, but I was certainly frightened by her. Her response was completely unexpected, disarming, and, I felt, could only mean bad things.

She finished the story and said, "There, wasn't that a good story?"

I wrote:

It wasn't good the first seven readings and the eighth was no different.

"My, but aren't you the little critic." She got up from the rocker and put me in the crib. "Now, you get some sleep and I'll see you in the morning."

derivative

I dreamed that I was a big man and that I was working in a yard, trying to dig out a tree stump with a pickax. There was another man standing near me, watching, though he didn't have eyes. In fact, he had no face, but was just a featureless wash of flesh. He was trying to tell me that speech always subjectively includes its own reply.

I stopped swinging my pick and looked at him.

"What are you doing?" he asked.

"I'm trying to remove this stump," I said.

"See, I got the reply my question desired. If I hadn't asked, then I would not have gotten that response."

I said, "What if I said, 'Just don't stand there like a lump. Can't you see I'm trying to remove this stump?'"

He ignored my statement and I began again to swing the pick, throwing dirt high into the air. Very high into the air.

"For example," he said, "when Joseph says to Mary, 'I love you,' he's seeking in return the same message, 'I love you,' only with the referents of the pronouns reversed."

"Then, I suppose the same is true when she says it to him," I said, still swinging.

"Precisely."

"That could go on all day. What if he says, 'Tell the truth, Mary, who really knocked you up?'"

bedeuten

One midmorning, when the sky outside my barred window was overcast and dingy, Madam Nanna presented me with a stack of books. Nine, to be precise. They ranged from a textbook in fluid dynamics to a handbook of popular astrology to Carlyle's *Sartor Resartus*. She put them into the crib with me, then sat in the rocker and rocked and watched and rocked. I finished reading the first of the books and closed it. I hadn't noticed before, but Madam Nanna was timing me. I saw her glance at her watch.

There was a knock at the door and Madam Nanna got up and went to it. She opened it a crack and then disappeared into the hallway. I didn't get the briefest glimpse of whoever was there, but I heard his deep voice. I heard him say, "Fantastic!" and then he said, "How long?" And then he said, "All right."

Madam Nanna came back into the room all smiles and just sat in the rocker.

I gestured that I needed some paper and a pencil and she got up and supplied them.

Are you going to tell me what's going on?

"Don't you like the way Nanna is caring for you?"

Frankly, no.

"Don't you like the books?"

I looked at the books, then around the room, then through my window outside.

Take me outside.

"That can be arranged."

For whom do you work?

Madam Nanna just laughed and gave my head a pat.

ephexis

No Place for a Pig

Paisley Porkstein and his sisters Peggy, Polly, and Penelope Porkstein rode in the bed of a pink pickup. They were being transported from Paul's Porkorama in Pomona to the Big Pig Pavilion in Palisades.

While the pickup pressed on along the parkway, Paisley Porkstein poked his head up and said, "I'm feeling piggy? What's to eat?"

Peggy Porkstein, whose plaid panties peeked from beneath her putrid purple skirt said, "Pipe down, pipsqueak."

But Paisley Porkstein paid her no mind. He looked at his plain little sister, Penelope Porkstein, and asked, "Wouldn't a portion of porridge dispatch the emptiness in your potbelly?"

"Not another peep," cried Polly Porkstein, pulling up her pedal pushers.

Paisley Porkstein peered at the procession of pickups traveling parallel to them. He pointed and said, "That pickup is packed with pecks of peaches, pecans, and pears. If only I could reach over and pluck one."

"Not possible," said Peggy Porkstein. "Besides, that would be pilfering."

"Precisely," said Polly. "The police might plug you for swiping a pear."

Paisley Porkstein was positive though that pilfering one peach or pear or pecan from the pickup would not hurt. And when the pickups were packed tight in traffic, he pushed out his pig paw toward the pecks of produce.

"Please, pull back," little plain Penelope Porkstein pleaded, perceiving peril.

But Paisley Porkstein persisted, pushing and pressing his pig fingers while his plump piggy toes held to the pink edge of his own pickup, the prospect of the peach and its principal parts pleasing his popping eyes.

Penelope Porkstein pulled on her ponytail, she was so nervous. Polly Porkstein pounded her fist against the truck, trying to persuade her paunchy brother to pull back. Peggy Porkstein pouted and called her brother "pigheaded."

Paisley Porkstein pondered pulling back to pacify his sisters, but the other pickup pitched toward them and Paisley Porkstein saw it as his portal of opportunity and pounced with purpose on a peach. "I told you I would prevail, you pooh-pooher," said the prankish porker. "I now possess a peach."

Paisley Porkstein plied the peach from the pile and then plopped, with preterminal ponderings, to the pavement. The pig was about to panic as pickups and Plymouths and Peugeots passed by on the parkway, but the pungent perfume of the peach calmed him down.

Paisley Porkstein peered ahead to see Peggy and Polly and Penelope Porkstein disappear in the pink pickup from Paul's Porkorama.

The paunchy pig then picked a path through the pickups and panel trucks and Pontiacs until his plumpness was panting at the shoulder of the parkway. "Phew!" he said. "Not a pretty picture." Paisley Porkstein pondered his pitiful plight. "A particularly putrid predicament and all I got was this piddly peach. This is the pits."

Paisly Porkstein looked at the parkway and then at the roadside and saw it was planted with portulaca and pennyworts and periwinkle and he thought, "How pretty."

Then a pleasant pair of people in a puce Packard paused at the side of the parkway to peruse the put-upon pig. "This is no place for a pig," the pleasant female person said.

"Positively not," said the pleasant male person, whose potbelly protruded much in the manner of Paisley Porkstein's.

Paisley Porkstein presented the man with the pit of his peach and said, "What's to eat?"

"Perhaps we should take this porker home," the woman said. "He's positively precious."

"Perhaps," the man said. "He has no poncho and I sense precipitation. Let's transport him to our pad."

And so the pleasant people took the pathetic pig, one Paisley Porkstein, to their palace by the Pacific, which for the potbellied porker turned out to be paradise.

donne lieu

locus classicus

If I make a noise in the woods and there is no one around to hear it, am I real? How could I make a noise if I were not real? Is the noise real? Can the unreal me make a real noise? Can the real me make an unreal noise? Can the real me make any noise at all? Can there be an unreal thought? Can I prove there is a god by kicking a large stone? Have I written myself into existence or have I doomed myself to an unreal fictional planet? Am I Ralph or *Ralph?*

Suppose a cantilever beam of length Q and that it has one end built into a wall, while the other end is merely supported. If the beam has a weight of R pounds per unit length, its deflection y at distance x from the built-in terminal satisfies the equation

$$48TAy = R(2x^4 - 5Qx^3 + 3Q^2x^2),$$

where **T** and **A** are constants hinging on the material of the beam and the configuration of its cross section. How far from the built-in terminal does the maximum deflection occur?

mary mallon

Not only did Madam Nanna take me outside into the sunlight and fresh air, but she took me into the world. I was strapped helplessly into a buggy and pushed along the small, but bustling rues of whatever sleepy little town I was being held near. What Madam didn't know was that I had spent most of the previous night not reading, but writing note after note that read more or less the same:

Help me! I am a kidnapped baby and this woman is not my mother. We have no relationship beyond captor and captive. Please get help.

At every opportunity, and they were numerous, I would slip a note to someone. People kept leaning over my buggy and making faces while coming close to tickle my chin with index fingers. I watched Madam Nanna and when she looked away I slipped a note into a hand. And to a person, each would brazenly open the message in plain view of the Madam and read it aloud. Madam Nanna appeared unbothered by the whole business and would simply share a laugh with them. "His older brother," she would say, shaking her head.

A couple of people, however, though they didn't seem to grow suspicious of Madam Nanna, did display discernible discomfort with me. We strolled on; she began to whistle as I slipped into what I think was my first depression.

pharmakon

writing poisons truth
sophistry knows no station

The geometry of this text is more than metaphorical. This I say so that the reader will understand the direct spatial implications of the work. I *want* the reader to trouble herself over structural analysis. I want there to be questions about orientation and location, *dispositio* and *locus, praeceptum* and *datum.* The shortest distance between two meanings is a straight ambiguity. There are prime signs that are divisible by only themselves and one.

a plant emits a visual message
there is only one bodily posture
no gesture stands alone

anfractuous

His name was Billy Joe Bob Roy, Colonel Billy Joe Bob Roy, and he was commading officer of the Division of Exploitation of Potentially and Reportedly Trainable Mentally Exceptional Neophytic Tikes, DEPART-MENT Department of the Pentagon, reporting directly to the Joint Chiefs of Staff and the President of the United States. Colonel Bill Roy wore on his chest all two hundred sixteen Purple Hearts he had been awarded while "fighting the yellow threat" in Vietnam. The Colonel listed to one side because of his medals and both moved and talked as if he had experienced a mild stroke. The mission of the DEPARTMENT Department was to detect, isolate, convert, and exploit any gifted individual, especially children for service to the armed forces of the United States of America.

Colonel Bill Roy was six-feet-three-inches tall and broad in the shoulders. His shoes were shined to distraction and he wore glasses with dark, reflective lenses indoors and out. Colonel Bill flew his own F-5E Phantom II jet all over the country and had once received a reprimand for buzzing the tower at O'Hare. Now his fighter jet was parked in a hanger at March Air Force Base outside Riverside, California. From March he had taken a spanking new olive green "Hummer," driven north to Carmel where he and his team, the Tike Evaluation and Manipulation team, the TEAM team, had set up shop in the abandoned offices of a failed investment firm. The TEAM team of the DEPARTMENT Department worked around the clock tracking down leads and determining whether certain children were worth a commitment of government resources and time.

Colonel Bill never slept. Colonel Bill took his clothes off only once a day, to shower, and then put on a clean uniform. He did push-ups, sit-ups, and chin-ups in his uniform. He ran three miles and then swam six laps in his uniform just before his shower. Colonel Bill always held a pipe clenched between his very white teeth. Colonel Bill had a booming voice and he whistled his s's.

"How's the subject, Nanna?" Colonel Bill asked. He moved his pipe from the left side of his mouth to the right.

"He's coming along," said Nanna. "I think he's the one. He's truly gifted."

Colonel Bill nodded. "How long?"

"I can't say yet. He's resistant, but I've got him confused. He's terribly bright, but at least he's physically helpless. Sleep deprivation won't work, since he doesn't sleep. He doesn't care much about food. He loves books. He reads everything and he's very critical. He will not be easily tricked."

Colonel Bill had lowered himself to the floor and was doing push-ups. "Sounds like you've got things pretty well under control."

"Yes, sir."

"Twenty-seven."

"Are you going to want to see the subject soon?"

"You decide. Thirty-three. I think we should take it slow, as planned. You get him dependent on you and then we work him."

bridge

To scribble is to produce a mark that will constitute a kind of fuzzy mess that is in turn productive in the way of constructing obscurity, that my future dissipation in principle will not deflect from operating and from capitulating, and capitulating itself to scribbling and deciphering. For the scribble to be scribbled, it must continue to function and to be a fuzzy mess even if that creature called the author no longer receives blame or credit for what is scribbled, for what he appears to have marked, whether he is conditionally truant, or if the victim of self-inflicted death, or if in general he fails to brace, *avec* his unequivocally rampant and fashionable design or regard, the repletion and amplitude of his signification, of that very thing which appears to be scribbled "in his name."[2]

> *try, as you might, to in my absence read,*
> *but here am I, before you, now and in every line,*
> *like nobody with me in the balloon's basket,*
> *nobody alone in the stretched and empty time.*

---

2. To differ, sweet dog, sweet dog of light.
   To defer, when shallow is the night.
   To spell it with an A when an E will do.
   To call on senses, active, passive, and blue.

defer, ad infinitum, *to the fact that I am here,*
between every word, yet nowhere to be seen,
not a present being, but a trouble to your mind,
a scribbler, a mugger, obscure and obscene.

ennuyeux

deceit
deixis
descriptor
dead
divisio

Madam Nanna managed to stroll me through the village without anyone raising an eyebrow. It seemed, in fact, that she had made a favorable impression on nearly everyone and that I was everybody's darling baby boy. In one store, there was a television glowing behind the counter. The clerk watched, eating some kind of crunchy food all the while, and Madam Nanna browsed through a rack of blouses and such things. On the television screen, policemen were pushing and shoving, what the newsperson called "escorting" Dr. Steimmel, Boris, and Dr. Davis into a police van. A few steps behind them, also in handcuffs was Ronald the chimpanzee. Standing nearby were my parents and with them was Roland Barthes, a cigarette dangling from his lips. A reporter stuck a microphone in my mother's face.

"Please, whoever you are, bring our baby back to us. You can have everything we own. Just bring our Ralph back to us." She turned and buried her head in my father's chest.

My father said to the camera: "This monster, this Steimmel, stole our son. Now, please. Please bring him back."

Then the microphone was in front of Barthes, who smiled, said, "It's the doubleness of the matter that perturbs me. That a child, at least I believe he is a child, and so should you, should be abducted, then rescued by abduction, yet never rescued, because the second abduction, much like the second coming, if you think about it, is only abduction, and the child possibly for only an instant was free, in that synaptic space between the hands of the abductors, like the instant between having a thought and not having one—well, it must be very confusing and yet illuminating for the little fellow. I'm French, you know."

The news reporter said, "And there you have it, the bizarre story of a baby kidnapped from its kidnappers. Here is a photograph of Baby Ralph." The picture looked like any baby in the world. How could anyone recognize me from that? Mo didn't mention that I could read and write and that was the only thing which separated me from other very short incontinents. The clerk looked right at me and smiled.

"Cute baby," the clerk said to Madam Nanna.

Madam Nanna strapped me into the car seat in her station wagon and drove me back to wherever the hell I was being held. Back in my room, I found that I felt more relaxed, a state my captors were no doubt seeking to cultivate. I didn't think they believed that I would adopt the nurse as a surrogate mother, but it was clear to me that they were attempting to bridge the gap between us by a fostered dependence. In a way, I suppose, it was a necessary consequence of the intense and prolonged isolation, and the singular and sole contact with Madam Nanna was bound to nourish a kind of familiarity. I was like an inmate in a remote desert prison; if lost outside the walls, I would have to crawl back to the only place in the landscape that for me existed. Their plan was not without merit, but I was Ralph.

supplement

Writing, even in my little hands, was not dangerous, did not exist "in the place of," did not seek to address the "deficiency and infirmity" of speech and thought.[3] My writing was no threat to my thinking, no threat to my meaning (as it was *my* meaning) and was in no way oppositional to thought or internal language or any fixity of meaning. It was what it was and that was all it was because how could it, like anything else, finally, have been anything else?

---

3. *Grammatology,* that Derrida guy. A sick discussion at best, where writing becomes more than a capsule in space, but a warhead against language itself. "It breaks in as a dangerous supplement, as a *substitute* that *enfeebles, enslaves, effaces, separates,* and *falsifies.*" Thought must be freed from writing, the paradox is that thought requires supplementation to be distinguished from *nonthought* (whatever that might be).

Day 12, in the desert without water

I had no agenda. I had developed a set of values, not out of my living with my parents, and not from having observed peers and coming to understand what behavior was expected, but from reading. I understood the logic of decency, categorical imperative, and all other statements of the "golden rule" aside. "Don't shoot at me and I won't shoot at you" seems far less effective than "I'm not going to shoot at you." But then, of course, dead is dead. Giraffes got long necks and turtles got shells, but humans got *avarice* and *vanity* and *religion*. Death occurs for no other reasons. The three enemies of thought. Perhaps they are *nonthought*. At least, they are corrupted, malignant, putrid thought. Burros and elephants can smell water miles away.

libidinal economy

Colonel Bill was just pulling himself out of the swimming pool when Madam Nanna came up to him. He dried his hat with a towel and placed it back on his head and patted down his uniform.

"Good evening, Nanna," Colonel Bill said.

"Colonel, the boy has a photographic memory. And he's able to understand the most complicated scientific material."

"Yes?"

"Don't you see?" Madam Nanna said, staring at the way the Colonel's darkened uniformed hugged his muscular thighs. "He's the perfect spy. He can look at the plans for anything and understand them, remember them. Perhaps he can even make them better."

"Hmmm."

"Imagine it. Mother and child visit nuclear-arms factory and take the group tour. Child waddles off. Child sees plans."

"Does he trust you?"

"Not completely. He's still resistant."

"Okay. Very good." Colonel Bill looked at Madam Nanna's eyes. "Are you looking at my artillery, Nanna?"

Snapping to, "Why, no, Colonel."

"I think you were, you little vixen." Colonel Bill shook a playful finger in Madam Nanna's face. "You'd like to see Mr. Howitzer, wouldn't you?"

Melting somewhat. "Yes, Colonel, I would."

"Well, you can't." His finger was withdrawn. "Never mix business with pleasure, I say. And this sex stuff, well, it's business, finally, isn't it? I'd open up a barrage if duty called, but only if that business presented itself."

"Yes, sir."
"Very good, Nanna."
"Thank you, sir."

peccatum originale

Larynx

The great vessels
lie patiently
on either side,
the triangular box,
flattened behind,
the organ of voice.

The pomum Adami
is a vertical projection,
subcutaneous,
more distinct in me
than in my mother.

Her throat is smooth,
her organ lies narrow,
placed higher in relation
to her cervical vertebrae,

bounded,
in front, by the epiglottis,
behind, by cartilage,
it whispers,
it calls, it cries,
it makes those sounds.

exousai

"How is young Ralph this morning?" Madam Nanna asked as she entered my room. She lifted me and took me to the potty. She left me there while she got my meal together on the tray of the high chair. I had gotten good with my toilet and was pleased and comfortable with the lack of demonstrable praise from the nurse. In this regard, she was completing her intended mission. As I was bored with the room and the single relationship, I decided that I would cooperate, or at least give the appearance of cooperation, so that we could move on to whatever next stage there was.

So, while she fed me I smiled. I wrote polite notes to her, asking for certain foods, certain books, telling her what I thought of Frege and Husserl and Hjelmslev. And she responded by softening, in a rehearsed and totally unconvincing manner, and giving me what I wanted. I wrote panicked notes asking her not to leave me and even contrived a bogus journal, which I pretended to hide away in my crib beneath my pillow and new teddy, that gave the clear impression that I was pining for her company and protection.

last night was a very long night   where is my Nanna?   there are noises outside   frightening noises   maybe some other men are coming to get me   Nanna brought me *The Crying of Lot 49*   **it put me to sleep, but she brought it to me   i wish Nanna would not leave me**

vita nova

The sky was robin's egg blue, clear, with some woolly white clouds far off. I was bundled up in a little parka and I could still feel the crisp air. It felt good to breathe it into my throat and lungs. We had walked out through the front door of the building in which was located my bedroom. It was an office building and there was a blank sign where a sign that was not blank must have once hung. Madam Nanna let me out of the stroller and I ran around on the grass of the front lawn. She chased after and I squealed silently with mute laughter.[4]

There were a few passersby, but they were all on the other side of the street. Many cars traveled the road, one of them being the dark sedan and the two dolts who had grabbed me that night in the rain. They drove by again and again, from the north and then from the south, staring as they rolled by. Then a man in an olive drab uniform and dark glasses came walking along on our side of the street, turned onto the lawn, and approached us.

---

4. Mind you, this was all an act for the nurse.

"Hello, Nanna," the man said. "Who is our little friend here?"

"Oh, Uncle Ned," she said. "It's so nice to see you. Uncle Ned, I'd like you to meet Ralph. Ralph, this is Uncle Ned."

"Hello there, Ralph." Uncle Ned patted my head and smiled down at me. "He's a handsome lad."

"We're just out enjoying the day," Madam Nanna said.

I shied away from Uncle Ned, ever so slightly, and hid behind Madam Nanna's ample legs, hugging her hose and smelling baby powder from somewhere on her body. I stole a peek at their exchanged glances. Uncle Ned was pleased and offered Madam Nanna a quick nod. She smiled, a haughty, self-satisfied smile and reached a hand down to touch the top of my head.

Madam Nanna knelt to talk to me. She said, "Uncle Ned has a very special playroom with some very special toys and there are books there and pretty lights. Would you like to play in Uncle Ned's playroom?"

I looked at Uncle Ned and then at Madam Nanna and offered a cautious nod.

"That's good, Ralph. That's very good. We'll have to get you a treat for being so agreeable."

ephexis

I
N
C
O
R
R
E
C
T
L
Y

There! I have spelled the word incorrectly.

unties of simulacrum

Eve sat in her studio, in front of an easel with no canvas. She had no more tears to shed over the loss of Ralph. Now, her grief and pain were silent, gnawing inward. She asked herself why she hadn't kept Ralph's talent to herself. Was she afraid of him? Did she truly not know how to handle him? Was there some piece of her deep down that wanted the world to see her baby boy and what he could do? Was it in some small way pride that had caused this great loss?

Douglas was off visiting his little graduate student. Eve knew all too well what he was up to. Those late-night trips to the office to grade papers. Eve had seen her once. Douglas had been talking to her and when she spotted Eve coming, the little cow had skedaddled off into the main office and out through another door.

And now, the disappearance of Ralph had caused a thicker wedge to be driven between them. They didn't touch anymore and all conversation was strained. In bed at night, the accidental brushing of a foot against a leg resulted in the leg being moved away. There was a lot of sighing. The second one to awake in the morning would wait until the other was finished dressing and gone before rising.

Barthes had come back to California because he enjoyed the beach and liked being away from his mother and had been hanging around Douglas because he admired the way Douglas worshipped him. Barthes took to coming around unannounced. Eve didn't like that. The man was impossible to talk to. In fact, language barrier aside, even the simplest transaction in a market became a huge production for the man. If it wasn't his insisting that he could not possibly understand why apples had different names since they were, after all, all apples, it was because the line was too long or the store was too cold or the cashier was too surly or that the cashier didn't know who he was.

Eve sat there in her studio in front of the easel and in walked Roland Barthes. He paused at the door to light a cigarette and tossed the spent match out into the yard.

"Hello, Roland," Eve said, knowing that those would be the last intelligible words she would hear for some time.

But Barthes said simply, clearly, plainly, "Douglas is poking a graduate student."

Eve was not so much stunned by the news (as she had known it, but still to have it shoved in one's face was painful), but by the fact that Barthes had not simply uttered a simple declarative sentence, but one that had some meaning, and, no less, meaning in the world in which she lived. "Yes, I know," she said, staring at Barthes as if he might at any second explode.

"I have the greatest respect for you," Barthes said.

Eve eased off her stool and began to back away. There was something wrong. The man was making sense. Then Eve was taken by the fact that she was afraid because the man was making sense and the backwardness of it all made her even more confused. "That's nice of you to say," she said.

Barthes drew on his cigarette and blew out smoke. "He's in her apartment right now. I saw them go in."

Now, the image of her husband with that floozie up in her apartment, kissing and touching each other swam through her brain. It made her sick and she forgot about the strange man in front of her making sense.

"It's awful," Barthes said. "Let's go there."

Sudden anger swelled in Eve's chest and she slammed her fists against her thighs and said. "Yes! Let's go!"

"No," Barthes said. "It would be better to get even with him. We French have a saying. *C'est plus qu'un crime, c'est une faute.* You see, because Douglas is off doing what he is doing, he is not here and so he cannot stop us. Do you know what I mean?" With that, Barthes approached. "I'm French, you know."

Eve's knee found Barthes' groin rather easily. She then bopped him on the head with an empty coffee can.

Barthes said, looking up at her from the floor: "Discreet, but obsessed. What I mean by that, as much as any string of sounds uttered in a throat can actually mean something, is that situations become complicated by insistence on contextual anchors and moorings. And what if I were to write out what has happened here? Oh, what a lie that would be! Necessary and contingent, both at once, but then neither really."

Eve stood staring down at the man, realizing that she had knocked the sense out of him. But now that he was himself, she helped him to his feet.

tubes 1 ... 6

The playroom was twice as large as Mo's studio and it was, *interestingly*, located in the same building as my room. I couldn't see the ceiling as it was dark above. Most of the light in the room came from terminals and consoles and a few lamps. Screens gave eerie, greenish casts to the faces of the several people who were already "at play" in the playroom. Computers chirped and telephones rang, but when one of the white-frocked crew observed Uncle Ned's presence, they all snapped to their feet and looked his way. Our way, as I was in his arms.

"Ladies and Gentlemen," Uncle Ned said, "this is Ralph."

"Ralph, these people are your new playmates."

I gave Madam Nanna my best look of alarm and she offered a comforting nod and smile and mouthed the words, "It's all right."

Uncle Ned bounced me on his arm. I studied my face in the lenses of his glasses. Then I thought about my lunch of bananas and crackers and half a frankfurter and spit up on his uniform.

"Oh, for corn's sake," Uncle Ned said, holding me away from his array of medals. He gave me back to Madam Nanna. "Somebody get me something."

The crew scrambled around, searching for napkins and bottled water. I looked for the slightest break in at least one of their faces, but found none. Dabbing at his olive jacket with a hanky, Uncle Ned said, "Okay, everybody go back to your play or whatever else you were doing." When no one moved, he barked, "As you were."

The crew went back to their terminals.

In the center of the room was a playpen, much like the one I had had at my parents' house and exactly like the one in my room there with Madam Nanna. Beside it was a little sofa and piled high on the floor were books. Books of all sizes and thicknesses, soft- and hardbound. Madam Nanna carried me to the center of the room and placed me gently on the sofa. The chair was just my size. No adult could have sat on it. It was soft and perfect and beside it was a lamp, which Madam Nanna switched on. I grabbed a book, leaned back on the sofa, and began to read. There was a collective intake of air by the crew, but I ignored them and turned a page. One of them said, "I don't believe it." "He's just going through the motions," from another. And much to Madam Nanna's credit, she said not a word.

"Okay, team," Uncle Ned said, "let's get to work." Then away from me, he said, not knowing that I could hear him, "I want to know what makes the little bastard work. And I want that knowledge yesterday. Do you understand me, mister?"

"Yes, sir."

Uncle Ned then came back to me and Madam Nanna, where he stood over me at the sofa and showed me his teeth. He was still raking at the darkened spot on his lapel with the rag. "Nanna, I'm going to leave you and our little fellow here."

"Okay, Uncle Ned," she said. Then to me, "Wave bye-bye to Uncle Ned, Ralph."

I glanced up from the page of my book, considered offering him only a smirk, but did the prudent thing instead, I waved bye-bye.

117

äusserungen

A demon may be good, bad, or indifferent. I was all three. What good is a demon who is not bad? Why, he's no demon at all. And what is more frightening than a demon who is unmoved and unimpressed by his own evil? In fact, the scariest thought by those inclined to believe in demons is that there are no demons at all, that finally they are responsible for the evil they see, discover, perform. Therefore, demons are good. And a good demon is really, really bad. And an indifferent demon is as bad as it gets, which is good. Out of the *massa confusa* there must come evil, because without it, there is no good, or so the literature told me. The unconscious, however, is ambivalent, unfocused, even wishy-washy, and so knows no distinction between good and evil. This I knew from watching the words on the page, realizing that though those words were issued perhaps consciously by some writer, they were, once left alone, without consciousness, were indeed without conscience, and certainly no longer in any way represented the things that they, initially at least, were seen to be representations of. Even my notes to Inflato, now removed from their moment of creation and delivery, if saved at all, would have meant nothing like what they meant then, perhaps serving solely as some sign to my parents that I had not been a figment of their imaginations. Words, I decided, were worse than photographs in that way, that way of cutting off time before and after the image, worse because, at least in a photograph, the constituent parts did not turn up in every other photograph as the words did in writing.

This is what I thought as I watched the crew scramble around me, jotting notes, attaching electrodes to my temples and my little chest, whispering to each other, then laughing at themselves for being afraid of my hearing. I read a couple of books while they monitored my brain activity, then mapped the *loci* of my brain functions (a term I use in spite of my disdain) and at one point they all gathered around one terminal and oohed and ahhed while I purposely shifted my thinking from Nietzsche to Ellison to Lowell to Mailer.[5] I was open on the table, but I didn't care. I was in control of myself, therefore in control of my observers, and I enjoyed the feeling, which was not one of power, but comfort.

---

5. At which point, I took it from their reaction, there was little or no brain activity they could locate.

causa sui

If I ended these pages here, where would I leave you? The abruptness of the ending would in a fiction be disconcerting, baffling, and disappointing, but in a reality? And what have I done by suggesting this? Have I betrayed myself as a fiction, or, by the self-conscious admission, simply reassured you that I am indeed real?

"I tried to turn the handle, but—"

> *K-nock, K-nock*
> *Who's there?*
> *Ifaman*
> *Ifaman who?*

If a man grasps truths that cannot be other than they are, in the way he grasps definitions through which demonstrations take place, he will have not opinion but knowledge.

> *K-nock, K-nock*
> *Who's there?*
> *Ahyoushould*
> *Ahyoushould who?*
> *"'Ah, you should see 'em come round me of*
> *a Saturday night . . . 'for to get their*
> *wages, you know.'"*

subjective-collective

We see now, as in all scenes, notably foreshadowed, the specter of much that is to befall our hero, our autobiographer; the historical personification of which, as it painfully takes shape in this story, lies scattered, in misty and nebulous detail, through this laboratory and that, and those that come next. I was a curiosity then and perhaps forever, a rhinoceros at a church social, a dwarf on a basketball court, a hawk in a chicken coop. And there I was in the lab, under the scope, my heat and energy being measured, my blood being analyzed, my eyes watched, and all by rather cold, detached, uncaring eyes. At least Steimmel hated me, was afraid of me. These people, Madam Nanna included, had no genuine reaction to me, but only to my measurements. They put me through tests not identical with but very similar to those performed on me by Steimmel.

"What a memory," the female member of the crew of five said.

"Memory is no sign of intelligence," the tall, fat man said.

"Still, it's a remarkable faculty," said the short, fat man.

I hadn't yet written anything for them and they didn't mention it, though my ability must have been reported to them. Madam Nanna didn't say anything, but just watched and catered to my needs, bringing me bottles of juices, helping me with exceptionally large books, taking me to the potty.

I was amazed at how much I perceived the team as machines, extensions of their instruments and computers. I was shocked when their hands were not cold to the touch as they connected electrodes and other sensors to my skin. Finally, tired of the testing and the monitoring, I wrote a note:

Please allow me to demonstrate a talent of which you are, no doubt aware, and which you have been waiting to observe firsthand. I must tell you, that I admire your considerable patience.

"Remarkable."

"What do you have to say now?"

"I'm impressed."

"Me, too."

"How do we explain it?"

"Is there any way we can weigh his brain?"

"Not precisely."

"His chromosomal structure is normal."

"Site brain activity and AER and EEG are erratic."

"Why doesn't he talk?"

Let's get on with the pogrom.

"My god!"

"What?"

"Is it a misspelling?"

"I don't think so. Look at his expression."

"He can make a pun."

I felt not quite real, looking at their faces behind the green glow of their screens. I was no longer taken by my perception of them as cold and machine-like, but by my perception of myself as somehow unreal, intangible, a skiagram, a reflection.

"He's usable."
"Definitely usable."

ens realissimum

"There are no signs, there are only differences between signs."

Could it have been, I thought, at that tender age, that the representation was the thing? Was there a real me, a complete and original me? Or was I simply the sum of their measurements, the tally of their observations, the compilation of their conjecture? Madam Nanna smiled at me, but was she smiling at *me?* No, she was smiling at my performance. Was she feeding me? No, she was feeding possibilities and potentialities. In several seconds, I moved from indifference to hatred of Madam Nanna and Uncle Ned and even the crew, with their interchangeable faces and bodies and voices. But I also experienced something a bit more profound, and troubling, a stirring of self-loathing as I recognized my capacity for emotional response. The self-loathing was exacerbated by the fact that its very existence was ironic testimony to the very thing in me that I was finding so unpalatable, namely a disposition toward witless and illogical responses.

consummatum est

The Papuans apparently, from rather old geographies, mind you, have a tradition of eliminating several words of their language upon the death of one of their number. So, the language must grow smaller and smaller, finally, following this to its logical end, disappearing all together. Except that there must come a time when the words necessary to express the custom to young members of the tribe are not sufficient. Therefore, the tradition necessarily kills itself and so language survives, in spite of the assassination attempt. *ne consummatum est*

The Straight and Narrative

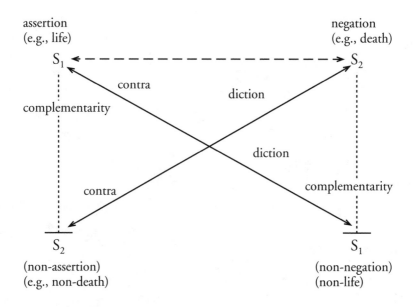

GREIMAS

E

différance

there is no such thing as digression

Tinnitus is a ringing sensation caused by some such condition as a perforated tympanic membrane or an excess of wax in the ear. It is a sound
heard only by the person with the condition, but it is a sound nonetheless,
however unobservable by another. This makes it much like pain, but more
interesting, of course, in that in all other matters we can hear, under normal circumstances, the same things. We never feel the same pain.

"I can hear the chicken," I say.

To which you respond, "I cannot."

I say, "You must be deaf."

You say, "But I can hear *you*."

"Then I must be imagining things," I say.

But of the ringing in my ears? I complain of it and you might say that I
should see a doctor about it. Granted, you might say the same when I
claim to hear an imaginary chicken, but you will not mean the same thing,
or at least the same doctor. The ringing is acceptable, as are after-images
seen following the lighting of a flash. But let the ringing become a voice or
allow the after-image to become a dog and you've got a problem.

there is no such thing as a non sequitur

Freud would have had me believe that a dream is a psychosis, one short-
lived, "introduced with the subject's consent and terminated by an act of
will." I dreamed of Madam Nanna and my mother playing tennis. Not by

consent did I enter into that dream. I sat there watching them pretend there was a ball and I, with them, pretended there was a ball. I even saw the ball go over the high fence. I ran and got the ball. By the absurdities and the *illogic* I am to construe that, during whatever time it took me to have that dream, I was psychotic. Perhaps I was (and perhaps I am), but not because of the nature of my dream. If my dream had no absurdities, the players being my mother and father, there actually being a ball, then would the dream not be a momentary psychosis? I was angered to the point of laughter as I lay in my crib contemplating that. In my dreams, I thought, it would be psychotic not to abide by the logic of that world. I imagined that I would not go to a costume ball and then complain about everyone's dress, or to an exercise class and protest because everyone refused to stand still. The dream is the thing until one awakes. And then it's whatever you want it to be. Much like anything else.

there is only authorial intrusion

There were once two philosophers who were sitting at the edge of a pasture observing a flock of sheep and commenting on their lack of wool. One smoked a pipe. The other wore red shoes. The pipe-smoking philosopher blew out a cloud of smoke and said, "I have a feeling there is no such thing as intuition."

subjective-collective

I was strapped into the all-too-familiar safety contraption in the backseat of the station wagon. Madam Nanna's head floated above the cloth upholstery by the passenger-side window. Uncle Ned's ample noggin drove the car. We were a picture from television, a Rockwell, an echoing, threadbare phrase. We started early in the morning, before sunrise, and we were headed south. I didn't know where we were going, only what I was supposed to do. The last readings given to me by the team concerned computers and the security thereof and thereabouts, which, even to their thinking, did not amount to much protection. I was supposed to find, look at, and memorize any and every blueprint, document, schematic, note, or telephone number that crossed my path. All I knew was that those kinds of things might be there.

We parked in a large parking lot dotted generously with palm trees. The trees were tall and straight, each having many dead fronds hanging down and wrapping the top of the trunk. Madam Nanna got out, opened the back door, and began to free me. She was wearing a pink dress, which softened her appearance considerably, though she was far from the picture I held of my mother. Uncle Ned was without his darkened glasses, his pale blue eyes exposed to the world, and he wore a yellow turtleneck beneath a kelly green blazer. As I understood the story, I was their adopted child, their having been unable to conceive after years of trying, doctors and operations and prayers. Madam Nanna carried me and Uncle Ned his briefcase. He was there for a job interview (wherever *there* was) and Madam Nanna was there to look around as well, to see the plant, to see the day-care facility in case she chose to take one of the many office-support jobs the firm was willing to offer company wives. All this I heard at the briefing, though I was not the real target of the meeting. My instructions were all too clear. *Look and memorize.* When possible, wander off into restricted areas and there, *look and memorize.* When held near the shoulder of someone reviewing or observing a document, blueprint, or computer screen, *look and memorize.* I didn't speak, so I was not required to pretend in any way and though they were all impressed by my intelligence, I was still a baby and they could not bring themselves to speak to me as anything but a baby. So, no one said, "Okay now, Ralph, you go in and pretend to be Nanna and Uncle Ned's baby. Give Uncle Ned and Nanna those looks you babies reserve for the people who feed you and give you stuff." All they said was, "Look at things, everything, and then you come back here and we'll play the remembering game. Okay, Ralphie?"

spacing

Dear Professor Townsend,

I thank you very much for the imposing number of off-prints you recently sent me. I admire your efficiency and I wonder how you are able to be so fertile in light of all your other work. During my down years I published very little. Now I have finished a book about Linguistic Traps and Psychological Types, which shall soon be translated into English. I just recently heard from a professor that universities are rapidly dismantling because mental workers are paid less than laborers. I have enclosed a typed text of my recent talk at the Symposium of the Aristotelian Society. Have to run now.

Yours Sincerely,

Jacques Derrida

libidinal economy

Colonel Bill, for no other reason than because he could, flew his jet fighter from March Air Force Base to Washington, D.C. and back, stopping for refueling at Strategic Air Command in Nebraska each way. There, while a crew of six men gassed up his *baby*, he sat in a doughnut shop and flirted with a waitress named Rita. He drank coffee, ate a cruller, and told Rita that he'd see her when next he landed there, giving her a wink as he slid off his stool at the counter and said, "Know what I mean?"

Back at March, the Colonel was met by Madam Nanna who was dressed in a crisp blue-skirted uniform.

"Speak to me," Colonel Bill said.

"He's a go. The baby's a go," she said.

"How does he work?"

"The team doesn't know how he works. They only know that he does work. He's truly remarkable. But there's nothing different about him. He's normal except for his intelligence."

"Then we can't replicate him. Is that what you're telling me, Nanna?" He slipped in behind the wheel of his Hummer.

"Yes, Colonel."

Colonel Bill stared ahead through the windshield and bit his lower lip. "But he's usable."

"Highly usable."

"Very good."

"How was the President?" Madam Nanna asked.

Colonel Bill turned the key and started the Hummer's engine. "The President is a fucking asshole, Nanna. He doesn't know his ass from that piece of shit who's his VP. Clumsy bastard, too." He shook his head. "Nixon, now there was a president. Sweaty palms, trembling lips, back-stabbing. Yeah, there was a President."

Madam Nanna stood away from the car. Colonel Bill looked at her as if for the first time, coming down from the apparent euphoria considering Nixon had created. "You're a fine-looking woman, Nanna."

"Thank you, sir."

"Why don't you come over here and sit on Colonel Bill's lap?"

"Yes, sir."

"There now. Isn't that better?"

"Yes, sir."

unties of simulacrum

Suppose I made all e's t's and all r's w's and all c's a's and all p's q's and all l's h's and s's n's and all o's k's and all g's d's and all i's u's and vice versa. Then water would now be RCETW. And suppose I made such substitutions throughout the alphabet. Would it still be English? Yep. Wchql rkihg neuhh nqtco Tsdhunl.

Language was my bed. More, writing was my bed. I felt safe in it. I needed it. I trusted it. I wrote notes to myself and read them. I wondered what they meant. I put notes away and tried to forget them so I could find and read them. I would tear them up and rearrange the words, read them backwards, read every other word.

Ysuwu dwu pn ywlbqx lp vlbylnp. Ysu dzynw lx pny audv.

degrees

The Weight of the Encephalon

My head hurts
the way it hurts,
weighing in at fifty-two
ounces soaking wet.

The pain weighs
as much,
just more than 3 pounds,
rolling like a great round stone
from floor to roof.

Fifty-two ounces,
an ounce for every card
in the deck.

Thirteen ounces
for every eight hours,

*during which I trace
the topography
with a match.*

seme

Madam Nanna was dressed *contingently.* What was it, I wondered, for a word to not *fit?* I observed often the space between the words at either end of the word in question. Was it size? The number of vowel sounds? Meaning? Madam Nanna was a *husky* woman. Not quite true. Madam Nanna was an *irksome* woman. Madam Nanna was colorfully attired. But, in fact, despite her clothing, was Madam Nanna that thing? Madam Nanna had and was wearing brightly colored clothes. Madam was *not* dull.

Of course, the fat Dumpty told me, a metaphor means nothing outside of its metaphorical context. Much as there is no sailing without a boat and water. Which is to say that the metaphor itself has no meaning. But but but but I was a confused tike, wondering how it was that a "stitch in time" made any sense to me without a context, until I realized that it didn't. So, if I speak of the *death of language?*

anfractuous

Inside the lobby of the Dionysus Missile Works, Uncle Ned was met by a tall man wearing tortoiseshell glasses. "So, glad you could come and look us over, Mr. Jones. I'm Mr. Chaein. We talked on the phone. And this must be your family."

"Yes," Uncle Ned said.

"This is my wife, Mary, and our adopted African American son, Jamal."

"Pleased to meet you, Mrs. Jones."

"Likewise."

"And right on to you, little fellow." Chaein shared a chuckle with Uncle Ned. "Right on," he repeated.

"I want to thank you for the opportunity to come see the plant and talk to you in person."

"Are you kidding? With your credentials? We're just glad you're considering *us*. I tell you what." Chaein signaled to a woman who was standing some feet away at a desk. "Let's get down to business. I'll show you the lab facilities and Lonnie here will show the little woman and the little *bro* around."

"Actually," Uncle Ned said, "I was hoping we could all stay together. You know, it would help us later when we're talking things out."

Chaein was slightly taken aback by the request, but recovered quickly. "That's fine, of course. Lonnie will just come with us to keep the wife company."

"That sounds great," Uncle Ned said.

"Lonnie, Mr. and Mrs. Jones and their adopted African American baby, Jamile."

"Jamal," Madam Nanna said.

"Yes, of course."

"What a cute little pickaninny," Lonnie said, pushing a wiggling index finger toward my chin.

We followed behind Uncle Ned and Chaein. The lobby was an explosion of glass and chrome. Chrome waste cans and glass desks and glass bricks and chrome rails along the stark white walls. Busy women just like Lonnie walked by carrying coffees and papers.

"I just love your dress," Lonnie said to Madam Nanna.

"Thank you."

"So, will you be looking to work here with us, too?"

"I haven't decided."

"Well, even if you don't, we'll see a lot of each other. We have a book club and a bowling league. What a cute little boy."

"We have the latest and best equipment," Chaein said to Uncle Ned. "If you need any piece of hardware, you just tell us and we can make it. You don't have to worry about anything. We have a Digitalis NX Logic Analyzer on every floor and networked to every computer on the floor. If you need more computer power, just say the word."

We stopped at a large window and looked through to a huge model of a town and surrounding landscape. There were hills and streams and rivers and houses and churches and little plastic people.

"It's pretty much northern Virginia," Chaein said. "Though we didn't have a particular town in mind. But it really upsets the boys at the CIA." He laughed for a couple of beats. "This is our HO scale Actual Impact Model, AIM. This is where we explode scaled-down versions of our bombs to observe the devastation. The model is 3-D computer-generated and it costs us close to thirty-seven thousand dollars to have the computer make a new one after each detonation."

Uncle Ned whistled.

"Not quite as good as blowing up the real thing, but we catch a lot less flack." He smiled back at the women and me. "Of course, this doesn't matter much to you, being a deployment specialist. What good are our little toys if we can't blow them up where the people are, right?" Chaein slapped Uncled Ned's shoulder. "The good old days of just flying over somebody and simply dropping one are all over. Now we need you."

Madam Nanna smiled at Lonnie and said, "My husband is a fuel-injection genius."

"You can say that again," Chaein said. "Fuel prices kill us. We've got to use less fuel to make using these things more cost-effective and that's where men like you, Jones, come in."

Uncle Ned hung his head shyly.

"Well, let's move on," Chaein said and led the way. He took us into a large lab where many white-jacketed men worked at computers. "Here's some of the support staff," he said. "Any blocks you run into, bring them here. Don't waste your time with calculations. That's what these people are for. We want you to be creative. What you do is an art[1] and we want to nurture that. I mean, what good is a nuclear device that just sits in your front yard? Deployment, that's the name of the game. I want you to think of Dionysus Missile Works as your gallery."

Madam Nanna moaned and said, "This child just gets so heavy sometimes." And then she put me down on the floor.

I watched the adults talk, Chaein and Uncle Ned about blowing the

---

1. Delacroix, Delacroix, Who's Got the Delacroix?:

   More than in any other European country, the slant toward didactics and the self-righteous was present in French painting. The predilection toward sermonizing in art appears early in the seventeenth century. Nicolas Poussin led the column through the trees and into the swamp. His painting *Et in Arcadia Ego* is a token of the amorphous. It depicts weary herdsmen reading the inscription on a grave marker, "I too am in Arcadia." The *Testament of Eudamis* is an examination of prudent submission; the dead citizen of Corinth leaves his friends the chore of feeding his mother and daughter. Antithetical epigrams of such preponderance could only have come from the French. The formal character of Poussin's art is Italian, though no Italian would have been so clumsy. The moralizing materializes in genre painting as well; Louis Le Nain's serfs are stiff and probably stupid, unfortunately not at all like the ruffians of Brower and other artists of the Netherlands. Religious paintings became very different from those done in Italy and Spain. The new direction in France was toward the spiritual life of the individual and the redemption for which no sane person could hope. *Grand goût* was riddled with self-righteous arrows and so too was the academic spirit of France at the time—the fundamental concepts of truth and right somehow having been shamelessly tied together. Reason and this desire to pontificate formed the *méthode classique,* represented in the seventeenth century by Poussin and the writer Corneille.

world to smithereens and Lonnie and Madam Nanna about the wives' tan-ing club. Then I waddled away, weaving between desks and past the backs of chairs and white-jacketed problem-solvers. I looked at screens and notes and did what I was supposed to do, *look and memorize.* A couple of men looked at me strangely, but I was a baby and they turned away and con-tinued their work.

Finally, the adults found me, all smiles and chuckles.

"Kids," Chaein said.

"He's a fast one, too," Uncle Ned said.

"In the blood," said Chaein and they all laughed.

Madam Nanna hoisted me up to her chest again and gave me a couple of playful bounces.

> *The pressure sensor possesses an inductive data transmitter attached to an electronic time switch in the control unit. Two evac-uated aneroids facilitate the moving of the plunger in the magnetic circuit of the transformer and so change its inductance. The throttle closed, the manifold absolute pressure is low, and the aneroids are*

In contrast to this heavy-fisted, ostentatious pose of the Wearisome is the second cur-rent, the Trifling. The Trifling was founded simply on *taste.* Of course, one is hard-pressed to say what a definition of taste might have been, but we can be assured that, in the final analysis, the taste prevalent in the Trifling was just as pompous and self-important as that of the wearisome. Early in the 1700s, there was a movement to make sentiment the criterion for artistic judgment. This was an escape from reason and morality, from the academic tradition, but of course it fell short of emotion or anything so genuine. What was of interest was the surface of reality. *Charme* and *esprit* were un-thinkable, pure essentials of a taste, the refinement and elegance of which could only have been fashioned in any of the world's more chic ghettos; both slaps in the face of reason and morality as well. By so-called definition, they are amoral. This absence from the sphere of moral sense was misread as frivolousness, bawdiness, and pornography, but actually it was only silly.

The appetite for the superfluous and inflated triggered the production of so many works of art that it is hard to get around the cumbersome of the whole of *esprit* to the rest of French painting. Watteau, Lancret, and others saw their paintings on the *rocaille* walls and ceilings of Parisian hotels in the first half of the 1700s. They were the delights of connoisseurs; others admired the floors. This decorative art, overstated as it was, was

dilated, moving the plunger out of the
magnetic circuit. The inductance is low,
giving a quick pulse.

incision

The question becomes, especially for one who chooses not to speak, whether there is a phenomenological value of the voice itself, whether it has any transcendence. Does the voice have an appearance? Can a voice be good? And does voice, the sounding voice, the speaking voice, carry the same impact as the voice of writing? And can the two work together or against each other, possibly even working to negate meaning altogether? A kind of complicity between sound and sign. I could change my voice even then, write them a baby note, a nasty note, a scary note. But it was always a note. The crew would look at it and ask, "What does the note say?" Never, "What did he say?"

bridge

"Hey, you can't leave me in here with this woman," Dr. Davis called through the rusty, but still-fast bars of the cell. She looked back at

---

thought to be a fleeting trend. Watteau, a front-runner of the school, was considered an accident, a deformed offspring of the Wearisome.

Certainly, the characteristic reasonless and unfathomable personality of the French people and their artistic sensiblilities beat with great life, but they cannot suppress the pompous components of French spirit. Rather, the play and lackluster battle between these contrasting elements give rise to French art. Between Poussin and Rubens lies a stretch of ground covered with the bodies of Frenchmen having fallen to bitter diatribes. We see a battle between tight-minded puritans on the one side and slovenly and probably alcoholic bohemians on the other. Ingres and Delacroix met in the dark alley of the nineteenth century, Ingres being convinced that Delacroix was a scout of the devil, and he the self-elected Norman Mailer of linearism and classical tradition.

Of course, essentials of the Wearisome and the Trifling could not resist spilling into each other and this is in major part responsible for the growth of French artists. Many of the artists, because of this, were severely impaired by paranoia and fits of multiple personalities.

Poussin and Corneille were long finished as symbols of French thought. Art had been muscled into submission by Louis XIV and company. The result: artistic impotence, limp brushes failing any effective strokes. The Academy strangled artistic life. The reaction, the revolt, was to seek complete freedom from academic shackles. But this illusion of emancipation or undisciplined and unrestrained speed-painting was

Steimmel who was sitting cross-legged on the bare mattress of the lower bunk, her eyes closed, her hair loose and wild about her face. "Hey!"

"Shut up," Steimmel said, her eyes still shut. "I'm not going to kill you. Not just yet."

"Guard!"

Steimmel opened her eyes and looked up at Davis. "What did you and that half-wit Boris think you were doing?"

Davis turned and faced Steimmel, braced herself by grasping the bars behind her back, put on a tough face. "Us? Why, you were going to try to keep that boy all to yourself."

"You're damn right."

"But you kidnapped him."

"What were you trying to do?"

Davis was caught short. "That's beside the point."

"No, that *is* the point. You know as well as I do what that kid could mean. All I needed was some time with the little bastard."

Davis moved cautiously toward the bunk where Steimmel sat. "Don't you see, that's why we should be working together. If we go at the subject from a couple of angles then we have a better chance of figuring it out."

Steimmel closed her eyes again.

---

soon prostrate on the battlefield of art history. Watteau, Lancret, and Pater faded early in the eighteenth century; they had exhausted all the *rocaille* walls and ceilings, the oppressive climate of self-righteous pomposity squelching them.

The vicious fascist tendency that now confronted the loose, speed-sketching mentality of the *petits maîtres* was essentially a reversion to the Wearisome, the self-important sermonizing art that had infected France in the classic period of the seventeenth century. This might have been termed neo-classicism or neo-Poussinism; the *grand goût* was back. But it had been tainted by a half century of subjection to the irrational and it was in need of the centurial dose of riboflavin and iron. Diderot said, "First move, astonish me, break my heart, let me tremble, weep, stare, be enraged—only then regale my eyes."

In the nineteenth century the winds of two old schools could be smelt blowing out of the past, the linear and the coloristic, though taking on new meaning because of the addition of Romantic and sentimental elements. While both schools incorporated these elements they continued to grow significantly apart. The coloristic and shamelessly ornate, by the 1830s, was manifested fully in the work of Delacroix; the French Romantic school. Opposed to this was the neo-classicistic movement with its narrow insistence on line and structure, different from the classicism of David in that it moved toward the saccharine and mawkish. Ingres led the way. The rudimentary difference between the new schools is not actually discernible, but the struggle between them was even sillier than the struggle between the Poussinists and the Rubenists of the seventeenth century.

"No, don't shut me out. Listen, if the two of us could work on the baby, then . . . well, who knows? Me and you, Davis and Steimmel, we could have that infant sliced, diced, and sacrificed to science in no time flat."

Steimmel opened one eye and looked at Davis. "Steimmel and Davis. But before I leap up and kill you, let me point out that not only are we incarcerated in the big house, the pokey!, the slammer!!, the clink!!!, but we don't even know where the little weiner wagger is!!!!"

"I know that. But what if we escape?"

"Escape? Are you out of—" Steimmel stopped and looked up at the ceiling and stretched her neck and back. "If a dumb, uneducated, redneck peckerwood like James Earl Ray can escape from prison, then why can't a couple of overachieving Vassar girls with Ivy League Ph.D.'s?"

"Now, you're talking."

$$(x)(Cx \rightarrow \sim Vx) \vdash (x)[(Cx \& Px) \rightarrow \sim Vx]$$

Back at the playroom, I was debriefed by the crew and Uncle Ned. I was sitting at the small desk, a notepad in front of me and Madam Nanna was sitting on the floor behind me, rubbing my little neck. No doubt, she was doing this to keep me loose so the information would flow easily. I regurgitated everything I had seen, but I placed nothing into context for them. Still, they seemed excited to see the equations and the phone numbers and the schematics. Their experiment had been a success, I gathered. I had understood from the beginning that the actual information garnered would be irrelevant, but what was of significance was the fact that I had effectively moved through the course and accomplished my mission. I *worked*. More, I was fully operational and functional. Uncle Ned was on the phone to the President immediately after my interview, telling him that the world was safe for democracy and baseball and that he could go play golf in Palm Springs with complete impunity.

Vexierbild

BARTHES: Do you remember when those felt-tipped pens first showed up on the shelves? I couldn't wait to get one home and try it out. They were made by the Japanese as well and if *they'll* use them to write . . .

HURSTON: I was dead by then. But also, who cares?

BARTHES: But don't you see? I'm talking about the action of writing. The gesture itself defines so much of the meaning, don't you think? I mean, even where I sit while I'm engaged in writing shapes my import.

HURSTON: What have you been smoking?

BARTHES: I have even observed what I call a "Bic style" of writing. You've seen it, those people who just churn out words endlessly.

HURSTON: (nodding) I do believe I have seen it.

BARTHES: I finally discarded the felt tip because the tip flattened out so soon. I'm back now to, and I think I'll stay with, truly fine fountain pens. They're essential for the kind of smooth writing I require. What do you use?

HURSTON: A sharpened bone and blood.

exousai

All of a sudden, I was no longer *Baby Ralph,* but Defense Stealth Operative 1369. I was no longer sleeping in the crib in my tacky little room, but in a bunk in a sterile, eight-by-eight cell with a toilet modified to accommodate my little keister and a guard just outside my door of bars. The little boy was growing up. There were no more novels for Ralph, only dry, technical, defense-oriented journals and manuals. No more strolls through the park, now it was policed parades across the exercise yard, the guard holding my hand while we walked to the far basketball goal, and then back. There were adult men, dressed similarly to me and there for reasons unknown to me, in the yard. I didn't know if they were DSOs like me or rapists and murderers. They were heavily muscled and tattooed. The guard wouldn't let them talk to me, but some shouted out, "Hey, look, baby meat!" and "What you in for?" and "What'd ja do? Take candy from another baby?" Finally, on the third day, I stopped and wrote on the pitcher's mound of the baseball field with a stick,

I am small enough to squeeze through the bars of my cell in the wee hours. Signed: **Paper Cut Mike.**

Why am I in here?

I asked Uncle Ned when he finally came to see me.

"Just trying to protect you, boy," Uncled Ned said. "You should know there are forces out there that will do nearly anything to get their mitts on you. Believe me, this is for your own good."

But a prison?

"Not just a prison, Ralph. This is a high-tech, state-of-the-art, maximum-security facility where some of the deadliest and most ruthless of the scum of society have been sentenced to spend the rest of their, hopefully, short lives. Why, even I, get the willies just thinking about this place."

I want some novels.

"No can do. You've got to be prepared at a moment's notice for any mission I dream up. So, it's the manuals for you."

I want to see my mother.

"I'm afraid Nanna has been reassigned."

My real mother.

Uncle Ned just looked at me as if I were crazy, as if he had no idea what I was talking about. "Well, you read those journals and I'll get you a lot more." He stood and looked at me. "My, you're growing like a weed, aren't you?" Turning to the door, "Guard, let me out of this stinking cesspool."

umstände

With a limited past, the present can only mean so much. Or so my reading would have had me believe. As I saw it, at least the quality of my experiences had run the range of any life, however long. I lacked volume, but bulk is probably, and perhaps necessarily, a bad thing. Uncle Ned was my sole contact to the outside world. The guard, who held my hand during my daily crossings of the yard, never said anything. He never even turned around to observe me in my cell, but just sat there reading fat novels about spies and sea creatures. I wrote him a note introducing myself and slipped it to him. He looked at it and, with an unchanged expression, folded it, and put it in his breast pocket. I observed him receiving orders, but never responding in any way other than nodding. He never made a sound, silencing my fellow inmates with glares and a show of his baton. I felt a closeness to my guard. Finally, I wrote him a note that read:

Please, would you help me? I miss my mother.

The guard read the note and for the first time looked me right in the face. He put his novel in the back pocket of his trousers as he always did before our walks across the yard, then put his finger to his pursed lips.

I nodded and watched him unlock my cell. He came in and wrapped me in a blanket, hoisted me up under his arm, and walked out of the block. He waved to a guard at the desk by the door, and in the locker room he stuffed me into a duffel bag with his smelly socks and dirty shirts. He carried me out and put me into a car, which upon being started made a whirring sound that some of my technical reading had allowed me to recognize as a failing water pump. I managed to work the zipper of the bag down some so that I could get some air and see out. I was in the backseat, again, and all I could see was a bit of bright blue sky through the window and the back of my guard's head. Hanging from the rearview mirror was a green figure of a tree and a white crucifix. He drove rapidly. I could tell by the way the car took corners and curves and it seemed that as his deed sunk into his thinking his driving became faster and more frenetic.

ootheca

It occurred to me that for those who spoke, the idea of silently speaking to oneself was not strange, but to me it made virtually no sense. I cannot tell you how I expressed my thinking inwardly, if even that makes sense, but it was not a matter of some inner voice finding some inner ear. The whole notion of the inner voice and the inner hearer raised the question of spatial orientation. If indeed there is no space between the two, then they are one, and it makes no sense to express either in terms of a contrary function to the other. I did not talk to myself, of course. But neither did I think to myself.[2] I think, I thought, I have thunk. I had no voice and Husserl would have perhaps suggested that for me there was no possibility of consciousness and for all I know that's right. For Husserl, I would have lived constantly with a broken proximity of the signifier (me) to the signified (whatever the hell I was thinking), since instead of speaking, I wrote, a gesture that somehow stood away from me. Whether that made me more or less vague or diaphanous, or standing nearer to or farther from my meaning and my self, I did not know.

How long is a memory?[3]

---

2. As the converse of that would be "to think to someone else." Perhaps this makes no sense when discussing telepathy, but that is, how do the *philosophers* say it, a special case.

3. Thank you, Mr. Kelly.

tubes 1...6

The guard's name was Mauricio, I learned when he walked into his house and his wife ran up to him and said, "Mauricio!" I was still in the stinking duffel. Then he pulled me out of the bag and she said again, "Mauricio!" Both utterances were complete sentences and meant nothing like each other.

"It's a baby," she said.

Mauricio, to his credit, said nothing.

"Is this the little boy you've been guarding?"

"Get packed," Mauricio said.

"Packed?"

Mauricio nodded. He was indeed a man of few words.

"Mauricio?"

"Hurry."

Rosenda didn't need the situation explained to her. She began to pack. I sat on the sofa and looked at the mute, but switched-on television across the living room. There was a picture of Jesus on the wall and the wallpaper was peeling just above it.

Rosenda was a short woman, a little fleshy, soft looking. I liked seeing her breasts through the thin white shirt she was wearing. I was hungry, but just then was not the time for a note. Especially with Rosenda already in a state.

"Mauricio? Where are we going to go?"

"Mexico."

peccatum originale

MO: So, what are you planning to do?

INFLATO: About what?

MO: I know about your little fling.

INFLATO: What fling?

MO: Don't insult my intelligence. You're not clever. In fact, you're clumsy.

INFLATO: I don't think this is a good time to talk.

MO: When would be a good time to talk?

INFLATO: I might as well tell you. I'm up for a job at the University of Texas.

MO: Hell, I know about that.

INFLATO: You couldn't possibly know.

MO: Texas called here because the third page of your vita was missing.

INFLATO: You didn't tell me.

MO: How could I? I didn't know anything about your applying. But I sent the page along anyway.

INFLATO: This stuff with Ralph—

MO: Fuck you. Don't use Ralph as an excuse. Ralph has nothing to do with this. I don't even think you miss him. I think you're glad he's gone. You were afraid of him.

INFLATO: That's not true.

MO: Yes, it is. As long as he was a dumb baby, that was all right with you. You were good at tossing him up in the air and shit like that. But as soon as he was on your level, above your level, you lost it.

INFLATO: I'm going to Austin for an interview on Friday.

MO: Great. I hope you get it. Is Bambi going to move there, too?

INFLATO: Eve.

MO: Go on. Please.

mary mallon

Colonel Bill paced the shag carpet of his Pentagon office, muttering, swearing, swinging a putter. He held his pipe clenched in his teeth and the words swam around it. He walked to his desk, slapped the button on his intercom, and shouted, "Gloworm! Get in here!"

The colonel's aide, Lieutenant Gloworm, stepped into the office and cowered by the door as the head of the putter narrowing missed his brow.

"Gloworm!"

"Sir?"

"What else have we heard from that goddamn maximum-security joke they call a prison out there?"

"Nothing, Colonel. The guard is missing. His house is empty."

"The guard, eh? What do we know about this man? I saw him when I was there, but I'll be a cow's teat if I can remember him. That's a bad sign. Not about me, but about him. Must be an enemy agent to be able to blend in like that."

"His name is Mauricio Lapuente. He's married to a Rosenda Paz. He was born in El Paso, but as far as we know he has no living relatives."

Colonel Bill pointed a finger at Gloworm. "See, there's a red flag. A fucking Mexican with no living relatives? Am I the only person who thinks around here? What about the wife?"

"We don't have anything on her. She might be from Mexico."

"I don't like this, Gloworm. You know what it makes me want to do?"

"What, sir?"

"It makes me want to fucking break somebody's neck. So, you get on the horn with those bastards out there in La La Land and you tell them to set up road blocks and send up heli-choppers and call out the dogs. But I want my little boy back! Do you read me, mister?"

"Yes, sir."

"Do you know what could happen if that little spook fell into the wrong hands and became a little spook for them? Why, it would be the end of the world as we know it. Now that anybody, no matter what they look like, can go anywhere they damn well please in this country, nothing's safe. And he's a fucking machine, Gloworm, a genetic freak. He's a baby who can read. He reads! That's enough reason, baby or not, to kill him. In fact, I want you to issue an order to our field operatives. I *want* that baby back. But if we can't have him, *nobody* can have him. You reading me?"

"Yes, sir."

Colonel Bill slipped his putter back into his golf bag in the corner of the office and muttered, "Goddamn monster baby on the loose. This is bad. Do you really understand the gravity of this, Gloworm?"

"I believe so, sir."

"And call Camp David and have my jet readied."

"Shall I call March and tell them you're coming, sir?"

"Hell, no. I'm not going to California. I'm flying down to Miami for the President's orgy. Didn't you get an invitation? Of course, you didn't. You're just a pathetic slug in the pecking order of life."

"Yes, sir."

"Now, get out of here!"

pharmakon

up periscope

There once was a man named Tod
Who believed he'd spoken to god.
He rode into town,
Spread the word around
And slept with a hooker named Maude.

There once was a hooker named Maude
Who slept with a disciple of god.
She did him up right,
Straight through the night
And when she awoke he was tod.

Q: Why is thought like money?
A: Because you can't take it with you.

ephexis

1

"I am not wherever I am the plaything of my thought;
I think of what I am where I do not think to think."

I had no problem with the Other, myself the Other, myself, or any bold line drawn between myself and the world, between signifier and signified and certainly, not for one second, was I troubled by a notion that in considering my conscious I-self that I was inhabiting or obscuring the line of any division between any of those things or my perception or conception of them. Blah blah blah.

If language was my prison house, then writing was the wall over which I climbed for escape. But climbing the wall either way meant, finally, the same thing, and so language was the prison and the escape and therefore no prison at all, any more than freedom is confinement simply because it precludes one from being confined. Indeed, my much regarded and remarkable relationship and facility with language had caused my incarceration, but also it had freed me, though I was still confined in the car of my new adults. I was still a prisoner to my size and to my inability to fend for myself. I was called a genius, but I was not. A genius, as far as I was concerned, was someone who could drive a car.

2

Ahead of us, cars were stopping and becoming a puzzle of steel. This made Mauricio very nervous and so he left that road and drove along a smaller one. Rosenda was terribly frightened and kept turning around in her seat to look past me out the back window. Then she looked at me.

"We have to stop and feed the baby," she said.

"We'll stop soon."

"And we must stop at a Kmart or a Target so we can buy him some clothes." She tilted her head and smiled. "He is a pretty baby. What are we going to call him, Mauricio?" She reached over the seat and touched my cheek. "We have been trying for so long to have a little one and here you are. It's a miracle, Mauricio." She looked at her husband. "So, what are we going to call him?"

Mauricio shrugged.

"Pepe," Rosenda said. "I think we should call him Pepe. How does Pepe sound, Mauricio?"

"Pepe," he said and nodded.

The likeness of their skin color to mine made us a proper-looking tribe. I could have been their baby. Mauricio drove us over a winding road, craggy slopes on either side, until we emerged from the hills before a plain of human activity. Cars swarmed and collected at intersections and at the mouths and anuses of parking lots. The afternoon sun was intense through the glass of the back window.

There was a shopping center and Rosenda was telling Mauricio that we had to stop. "Stop, honey, stop. We need things for our baby boy." Looking back at me. "Our sweet little Pepe."

I must admit that there was something like love in her eyes, but I was sickened by it. There was no subtlety, no understatement, no refinement, just wide-eyed, sloppy, indelicate adoration.

"Go," Mauricio said.

"Aren't you coming in?" Rosenda asked.

"We'll wait here."

"No, Mauricio, it's too hot in the car," she complained. And she was right. I was sweating on the vinyl seat. I was thirsty. I was hungry. I had to pee. Rosenda added, "Little Pepe probably has to go potty." What an unfortunate expression. She was out and opening the back door. "Come on, li'l Pepe."

supernumber

You don't know Polk County lak Ah do.
Anybody been dere, tell you de same thing too.

My mother was crying somewhere and not entirely for the loss of me, but for every wrong turn of her life, my father being the most glaring token of her misguided journey. She was sorry she had ever had me, but loved me no less for the regret. She would not have given up my life to negate her mistake, and she would have given her own to have me back again with her. Instead of my face serving as a painful reminder of her unfortunate encounter with the man she so despised, his face conjured feelings of loss and guilt as it made her think of me. She was crying somewhere because she thought she was a monster. She was crying somewhere because she was not sure she wanted me back. She was crying somewhere because time and space and language had cheated her badly. And finally, she was crying because, since my loss and since her severance of connection with my father, her painting had gotten good.

> *ergon*
> *eidos*
> *emic-etic*
> *event*
> *everywhere*

vita nova

Mauricio pushed the cart while Rosenda toted me through the aisles of the store. No one gave us a second look, though a few women offered the customary baby-waves to me. I returned my customary sneer, which I had resigned to believing was seen as simply an odd smile. The people passing were set phrases, mechanically repeated every few seconds and becoming comic for it. Finding it funny, I started to smile and as I started to smile, more people paid attention to me, pointed and smiled also and so it became funnier . . . You get the idea. Until the whole store was abuzz with talk of the good-natured baby in the toddlers' clothes section. People came

147

over just to see me, playing peekaboo behind racks of down parkas for teenage girls, waving to me with wiggling fingers over displays of towels. All of this made Mauricio very nervous. Rosenda, however, loved it, and bounced me conspicuously against her ample teats. It was hilarious and I couldn't stop, what constituted for me as laughter, smiling. The scene in the store had become a revolution of sorts. Clones of clones chasing the three of us through the aisles, Mauricio pushing the cart filled with a set of pajamas, a little toothbrush, some big-boy underpants, six T-shirts, three pairs of sweatpants, and a pair of sneakers, Rosenda trotting behind him, hoisting me back into position every three strides. Mauricio was perspiring and Rosenda was by now nervous as well. I was tired of it all and no longer smiling. And so, people took to making faces, attempting to return me to my good mood. Instead of sneering and running the risk of being misunderstood, I turned away from them all and buried my face in Rosenda's neck.

Mauricio fumbled with the keys once we were back in the car. This time I sat in the front on Rosenda's lap.

"Hurry," Rosenda said.

"Okay," Mauricio said.

"Hurry," she said.

"Okay."

"Mauricio," Rosenda said.

"Okay."

Conversation is a messy business at best.

Lost in Place

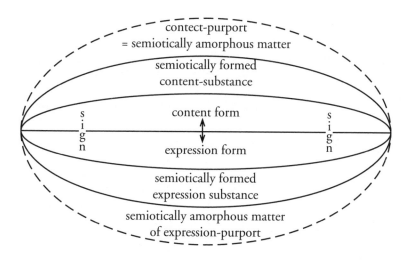

HJELMSLEV

F

différance

1

Clockwise is a direction and so is south, but if one continues in a clockwise direction no progress will be made. And no one ever comes from clockwise, though people often turn south or to the south or from the south. The words on the page always travel in the same direction, whether left to right or right to left or up to down or, as in the case of short-cut seeking, bad poets, clockwise or counterclockwise in the shape of a gull.[1] But there is no direction simply because the words are on the page and meaning knows no orientation and certainly no map. Meaning is where it is and only where it is, though it can lead to anyplace. Confusion, however, is necessarily only in one place and looks the same regardless of where it stands in relation to meaning. Being confused always looks the same and it comes from clockwise.

2

From shopping, Mauricio drove us down the road to a restaurant where we sat in a booth in the back near the kitchen door. The waitress came and said something baby-friendly to me, then to Rosenda and Mauricio, "My name is Trudy, if you need me." And I thought, "and even if we don't."

---

1. I have neglected here to mention from interior to exterior (or the reverse) because as I see it, there is no inwardness to my expression and so there can necessarily be no outwardness. There is no exteriority of the signifier or the signified. There is no absence to presence, no difference to sameness.

Rosenda ordered fruit and crackers and milk for me. I didn't protest. I was starving. I actually enjoyed the intensity of the desire. But I never got to eat. The burning in the pit of my middle made me consider, through my discomfort, a connection with the world, wondering where bananas came from and what kinds of boats transported them.

3

Is there a circularity that has us pass into the *other* indefinitely? Are we in fact changed by the nonchange that traveling forever in a circle creates? Is a change of orientation, but not of spatial location, a real change? As I circle the bee on the flower with my net and the bee dances around to continue facing me, do I ever really get around the bee? With all the movement, there is no movement. For all the repetition, nothing happens. The circle displaces change, and this change from the presence of change becomes the absence of change, becomes negativity, nonbeing, lack, silence. Counterclockwise.

ephexis

What am I doing with this child? My wife is thrilled that he is with us, but what am I doing? He is trouble. What was he doing in the prison? Is he a devil-child? I thought I was helping. He wrote me a note. How could he write me a note? He's a baby. It took me a long time to get that job. That was a nice house. But a baby shouldn't be locked up. It is not right for a baby to be locked up. But why was he locked up? Maybe he is a devil-child. Rosenda is so happy, though. A devil-child could not bring such happiness. Where are we going to go? That man who would come and talk to the baby was important, from the government. I could tell by the way I was no one to him. He was afraid of the baby. I could tell that, too. Maybe he is a devil-child. Or maybe the devil wants him.

My poor Mauricio, he is so scared. He makes me scared, too. It is a miracle that we finally have a little one. So long we have tried. I have prayed and prayed. I wonder why he was in the jail? He is a beautiful baby. His eyes tell me he is very smart. I hope he is smart like my Mauricio. I hope we can find a place where Mauricio will not be afraid. I hope we get to Mexico soon. My little boy. He is so beautiful. I loved him the moment I saw him for the first time. He is a miracle. I will protect him.

ootheca

Humans invented language. So says the innocent. Language invented humans. So says the cynic. My parents made an offspring. Or was it the case that I made them parents? There I was again, making parents of people. Chicken? Egg? Omelette? The beginning of sense is to realize that the term *sense* is a stand-in for whatever *sense* can be made within a particular context, just as *thing* serves for any noun substantive, just as *quality* serves for some adjective. *Aliquid pro aliquo.* To say that in some sense that thing has a certain quality means nothing, except here where it works to make my point. *He was making sense* tells you nothing of what he was saying. *He had a certain quality. He came in waving this thing.*

I was sick of the whole mess. I had no private language,[2] but language for me was, in the strictest sense, a private affair. Somewhere the government was seeking me, but of course they could not make it public. They could have perhaps intensified their hunt for the missing Townsend baby, but that would not have served them. I was safe to that extent from any outsider turning me in. It being the case that no normal person would have been able to recognize me from the poor photograph so briefly flashed on the television two or three times.

Mauricio and Rosenda sucked up all the food that came to the table while managing to shove a banana and a bottle of apple juice down my throat. Watching them eat was a bit frightening, hands constantly reaching, jaws constantly working, lips smacking. Fried potatoes dipped in blood red sauce, grease dripping from buns and fingers. Their napkins were balled up and good for nothing at the end of their exercise. Rosenda slurped up the last of her frothy drink and smiled at me with a white mustache.

"How's my li'l Pepe?" she asked.

Mauricio looked at me, but didn't smile.

Outside, Mauricio paused before getting into the car. He seemed to listen to the wind. Then he fell in behind the wheel and looked back at me.

"What's wrong, Mauricio?" Rosenda asked.

Mauricio just shook his head and squeezed the steering wheel, staring ahead through the windshield. "Need to hide," he said.

"Hide?"

---

2. Anything you want.

"Looking for us."
"Where are we going to go?"
"Father Chacón," Mauricio said.
"Father Chacón?"
"Father Chacón."
"I think dinner made me sick, Mauricio."

derivative

The Epigastric

The stomach before,
filled with sweet air,
supplying all that
lies in the cavity,
sitting

before the aorta,
the diaphragm,
expanding
with the motion of life,
it surrounds the cœliac
axis

and root
of the mesentric artery,
downward to the pancreas,
outward to the suprarenal
capsules,

receiving small and large
slanchic nerves,
semi-lunar ganglia,
on either side,
squeezing breath.

subjective-collective

Drs. Steimmel and Davis were being transported from the federal holding facility to what they were told was a remote federal reformatory, which was no reformatory at all, where they would have no contact with anyone, especially the press because they had not only witnessed the capabilities of a particular baby, but might also be able to piece together who might want him and why he might be wanted, and told also that the society was simply fed up with miscreants who sought out and made victims of children, that people were sick of having to be reminded of the problem with every use of milk from a carton and so they, Drs. Steimmel and Davis, were going to be put away, out of view, without a trial, without due process, without a second thought, but Steimmel and Davis were not concerned with this because the child still lived and was out there somewhere, waiting to be studied, waiting to be figured out, waiting to serve their desire for scientific fame and immortality, out there in the world, though they were in shackles, shuffling their feet through a long corridor from their cell, single file, toward the heavy door that led to the loading dock and to the yellow van that would take them to a helicopter that would in turn take them to a bastille that no one outside of the U.S. Justice Department and the FBI had ever heard of, Siberia, St. Helena, where they and, no doubt, Boris and perhaps even Ronald the ape, would spend the rest of their lives, reflecting on freedom and the days when they were so close to unlocking the secret of language and on the threshold of fame, where they might in time turn to each other or to whomever else the government had seen fit to lock away in similar fashion, seeking all those things that people need in a life, love, affection, struggle, sympathy, and scorn, especially scorn, because scorn was perhaps the most close-making of human feelings, it being, even in art, the one thing that brought audience into the work, and so in science, Steimmel thought as they closed the yellow van doors, her wrists chained to her sides, Davis beside her on the metal bench, the male guard across from her, not in a uniform but in a brown suit, his black pistol sheathed on his worn belt, staring ahead at Steimmel's face, but not reacting nearly quickly enough when the desperate psychoanalyst threw her body across the space between them, her head leading the way, her skull feeling as though it might crack and split wide open as it struck the man's chin, driving his jawbone up into his brain and causing him to black out so that he fell over and Davis reached into his pocket, found the key, and undid their cuffs and leggings, Steimmel pulling free the man's pistol and testing the weight of it in her hand, glancing forward toward the van's cab, thinking, then chanting, "Brute force, brute force, with all our brains, brute force."

peccatum originale

Colonel Bill flew his Phantom south and landed on the U.S.S. *Theodore Roosevelt,* which was floating idly in the ocean off Miami. He climbed down from his cockpit and was given a gift by an adoring young sailor, a blue cap with the insignia CVN 71. Colonel Bill, however, barely acknowledged the gift, and the young sailor not at all, but he did toss a salute up to the ship's commanding officer before boarding a helicopter that would take him to Key Biscayne and the President's orgy to which he so looked forward. From the helicopter, he looked down at the water and the approaching land, the helipad, and the sprawling complex of buildings. Where was that boy? He shook his head, stymied, angry at himself because he did not quite know how to proceed. But there was the President's party below and that would at least take his mind off his problem. There would be women down there for the using. Maybe some of them were even enemy spies who had sneaked in hoping to gather secrets during intimate moments or while a senator or a general slept and talked in his dreams. He was excited by the prospect. He defied any of the commie bimbos to make sense of anything he said, awake, asleep, or climaxing or drugged into a stupor by a deftly planted Mickey Finn.

The helicopter landed and Colonel Bill held his hat in place until he was well clear of the blades. He was met by a server with a tray of glasses of champagne and a slight man in a suit. Colonel Bill sipped a glass of champagne.

"The President is very glad you could make it, Colonel," the suited man said as they walked toward the house.

"The President can't wipe his own ass," Colonel Bill said.

"The President would like a quick briefing on the baby situation."

"The President can go put his tongue on an ice tray for all I care. Are you reading me, mister?"

The suited man stopped. "Mr. President," he said.

Colonel Bill snapped to attention and slapped his forehead with a salute. "Mr. President, sir!" he barked.

The President stepped down the steps toward them, tripping on the way and being caught by Colonel Bill. "Thank you, Colonel. I'm going to have to get that step fixed. Glad you could make it."

"You wanted to talk about the baby matter, sir?"

"Oh, yeah. Is the baby still lost?"

"Yes, sir."

"Okay. Now, let's go have sex with young, simple-minded women we'll never see again after tonight."

supernumber

1. Laura stands in the kitchen of her apartment. Douglas looks older to her now than he did the first time she kissed him. She looks at how his stomach pushes at his belt. She folds her arms and leans back against the refrigerator.

2. Douglas feels Laura staring at him. He says, "Austin is a great town. They tell me there's a lot of great music there. Is there anything you'd like me to find out about the program?" When she just looks away, he says, "I leave for the interview tomorrow."

   "It's Texas," she says.

   "So?"

   "Why would I leave California for Texas?"

   Douglas sits in one of the ladder-back chairs and holds his face in his hands.

3. Clyde is stunned by Eve's new paintings. "I can't believe it," he says. He walks around the room and then steps back from a four-by-five-foot canvas rich in blues and greens. "I have no idea how you did this. The composition, the color, the texture. It's all here." Clyde sits on Eve's stool, rubs his eyes. He is moved by the work. "I was expecting the work to be, you know, sad or something. But it's not. It's full of pain, but it's so alive. I'm sounding really corny."

4. Eve walks over to Clyde and kisses him on the mouth.

seme

Rin instead of *run*. The verb "to run" seems to run into itself. On the one hand, it indicates movement as in foot before foot, speed; on the other, it expresses interposition of waiting, the interval of *spacing* and *temporalizing* that exists between the beginning of the verb and the end of it. So, the word is stationary and moving, at once. *Run* and *ruin* are very close, the only difference being "I" and therefore, it is the "I" present that ruins the run. And so, *run* becomes *rin,* and *rin* is neither a *word* nor a *concept.* In the one case *run* requires a subject, but does not signify identity and so must signify nonidentity, but *rin,* by the very presence of the "I" not only signifies identity, but also nonidentity, as it requires no subject. So, we give the name *rin* to the movement that is no movement, a response to requirement of subject in the sense of *run,* which by the addition of "I" becomes *ruin.* But, of course, all this works only if I exclude "U."[3]

Vexierbild

> *Seven men*
> *can be obliterated,*
> *burned or hanged*
> *or drowned in a lake*
> *and forgotten.*
> *Men gone, but*
> *not seven.*
> *Seven men lost,*
> *but not seven.*
> *Seven is, will be.*
> *All men will die*
> *but not seven.*

Night fell while we were in the restaurant. A chill came with the darkness and Rosenda bundled me up in her acrylic sweater for warmth as we walked to the car. She sat in the backseat with me and sang softly while Mauricio drove.

"I hope Father Chacón is there," Rosenda said softly, thinking that I

---

3. But suppose we *trace,* if you will, the steps of *rin* and the footprints of *run* and what this leads us to is the fact that there can be no *rin* without *run* and there can be no *run* without a subject, "I" making ruin of it and so, at least "U" is necessary. So, *rin* is dependent on the presence of "I" and "U."

was asleep. I was feigning sleep to make her shut up. "We haven't seen Father Chacón since he left Monterey. Why did he leave there?"

Mauricio grunted an acknowledgment of her confusion. "Asleep?"

"Yes, our li'l Pepe is sleeping."

Steimmel and Davis hand- and ankle-cuffed the driver of the yellow van to the unconscious guard in the woods by the side of the road, the chains of the shackles passed around a small but sturdy tree.

"I don't believe it," Davis said, nearly jumping up and down. "We've done it. We've escaped."

"You might as well kill us," the driver said. "You're in that much trouble."

Steimmel lowered herself to a knee and looked the man in the face. "Why in the world would you say something that stupid? What if I believed you? Then, I'd shoot you. You don't really want me to shoot you, do you?"

The man was frightened by Steimmel's eyes and the evenness of her voice. "No," he said.

"So," Steimmel said, "you said that just to hurt me in some way. To hurt my feelings or to ruin this escape for me. Is that right?" She waved the barrel of the pistol in his face.

The terrified man nodded.

"That hardly seems nice. Does it seem nice to you, Davis?"

"Come on, let's go," Davis said.

"Please don't shoot me," the driver said.

"Oh, now, you don't want me to shoot you." Steimmel stood and looked down at the man. "You little prick," she said. "You cowardly piece of crap." She pointed the barrel of the pistol at him.

"Come on," Davis said, again. She was looking at the road. "Before somebody comes."

The doctors climbed into the van and drove away.

Colonel Bill's penis was inside the vagina of a woman whose name escaped him. He was about to ejaculate when the woman said, "You feel good for not having a big one." This caused the Colonel to stop all maneuvers and sit up.

"What is it, sugar?" the woman asked.

"He's out there. My baby's out there and I've got to find him."

There were three children and they were standing around discussing how they attributed credit for their achievements to their parents.

The first said, "I draw a circle and throw my achievements up in the air. All that land outside the circle are my parents'."

The second said, "I draw a circle and throw my achievements into the air. All that land inside the circle are my parents'."

The third smiled, said, "I draw no circle. I throw my achievements into the air. And that's where they stay."

Father Chacón was a plump man. He met us at the door of the mission, his collar tight about his red neck. He was bald on top with hair above and behind his small ears. His hands were thick and short fingered and he kept wetting his lips as he spoke. He referred to himself in the third-person and never stopped smiling.

"Come in, my children, come in. Father Chacón always has time for you. Why are you so agitated? Tell Father Chacón."

"We have a baby," Rosenda said, sitting with me in her lap. "A new baby boy."

"Father Chacón sees. What a beautiful little child."

"The child is not ours," Mauricio put in.

Father Chacón looked at him.

Rosenda reached up and took her husband's hand. "Mauricio freed him from prison. We call him Pepe."

Chacón stepped to the window and looked across the yard to the road.

donne lieu

> *figura*
> *facultas signatrix*
> *frequency*
> *fable*
> *fuzzy*

I may in my own analysis of my work here, if a thing can indeed be an analysis of itself, divide the signifier, which in this case is not me, but the text itself and follow the analysis as I follow the text, the material text being comprised of units and sub-units, lexia and sub-lexia, my sections designated by capital letters and sub-sections by headings and even whatever numbered units therein, down to sentences, to words, to letters, what one might call reading units (when one has nothing better to do). Is the division arbitrary and if so, is any of the meaning likewise and so without purposeful implications beyond those specified by the undivided signifier that poses only conspicuous problems?

If I may, I say that I am a complete reading system. My meaning is exactly mine and I mean only those things I seek to mean, all other possible meanings having been considered and sifted from the material whole. I assert that no other reading than the one I intend is possible and I defy any interpretation beyond my mission. To seek that meaning is to serve and work with my system. This is my language and only mine, my units, my pieces, my game. However . . .

degrees

The kiss hadn't gone well, Laura's mouth not quite softening and her lips failing to part. She remained leaning against the refrigerator in her kitchen and Inflato pulled away from her, looking out the window as he backed up until he bumped into the stove.

"I'll bring you something back from Austin," he said.

"That'll be nice," Laura said. She tugged at her short skirt.

"I was just thinking. What if you came with me? You could look around and maybe have a little vacation."

"I don't think so, Douglas. I've got to finish that paper for Thiebald and plus I've got student work to grade."

"Yeah."

"I hope it goes well for you," she said.

"Yeah."

Inflato turned and stepped toward the door. "Maybe I'll give you a call when I get back."

Laura came to the kitchen door and watched him.

He opened the door and left the apartment. He stepped down the hallway and started down the stairs, moving to the side to allow another man room.

"Hello, Townsend."

"Hi, Roland."

ennuyeux

I sat on the potty while Rosenda watched. A sad scene, but I had grown accustomed to such indignities. As I sat there, ignoring the woman, I closed my eyes and considered my mother. Actually, I considered Lacan, as was my wont when doing what I was then doing. At that moment, I contemplated his restatement of the Freudian Oedipus Complex. That I as a male child should identify undividedly with my mother and her desires in an attempt to complete that which was lacking in her was, at least, a rankling notion, but to proceed from there to my identification with the phallus as the object of my mother's desire and in so doing present myself as a mere erasure, why that served to make my insides flip about. And so the exercise of considering Lacan facilitated my defecatory mission.

"Very good," Rosenda said. "You made a nice big poopy in the potty. A big-boy poopy. I'm very proud of you."

Rosenda carried me back out to where Mauricio was telling Father Chacón the rest of the story. The priest looked at me with a big smile when I returned. He looked to Rosenda and said, "We can't very well let anyone put a child in prison now, can we?"

"So, you'll help us?" Rosenda asked.

"Of course, Father Chacón will." He reached over and put his fleshy palm over my head. "Why don't you take little Pepe into Father Chacón's room and put him down for a rest," he said. "Father Chacón will get us some food."

In the bedroom, I looked at the walls, wondering what they might tell me about the fat priest. There was a crucifix, which was no surprise. There was a larger calendar that had above the days of the month a photograph of lavender bearded irises. And there were two sketches of young boys in uniforms that I recognized from my reading of my father's back issues of *Boys' Life* as Cub Scouts.

pharmakon

"Give me another one," Douglas said to the bartender. "Do you understand women, Charlie?"

"Name's Phil."

"Right. Women." Douglas shook his head. "You ever been to Texas?"

The barkeep wiped down the bar, then put the rag away. "I was in Houston once."

"What about Austin?"

"Never been there. I hear it's a nice place. I'll bet it's hotter than the devil down there."

"I'm going there for an interview. Might be moving there. My wife, however, isn't going." Douglas ate a handful of popcorn and looked over at the door, saw the daylight outside as someone left.

"Sometimes it works out that way."

"Right. You got kids?" Douglas asked.

"No."

"I had a kid. He got kidnapped."

"No shit." The bartender leaned forward and rested on his elbows.

"Yep. A fucking shrink stole him and then somebody stole him from her. Pretty wild, eh? I didn't like him very much."

"What are you saying?"

"My wife is a painter. Set me up again."

"Why don't you go home?" the bartender said.

"Haven't you been listening?"

$$(x)(Cx \rightarrow \sim Vx) \vdash (x)[(Cx \& Px) \rightarrow \sim Vx]$$

Father Chacón came into the room. I was lying on the bed wide awake and he was talking to me as he approached. "Little Pepe, poor little Pepe. You're very lucky that good Catholics like Mauricio and Rosenda found and saved you from the devils outside. To put a baby into a prison is evil." The fat man sat on the edge of the bed. "But you're safe here in this sanctuary. This is a house of God and you're safe here." He put his hand on my leg and I could feel the heat of it through the material of my trousers. "You'll stay here for a while. Perhaps, Father Chacón will even suggest to Mauricio and Rosenda that they leave you here with Father Chacón where you will be safe from the forces outside, the forces beyond the walls of this sanctuary." He nodded and patted my leg. "Father Chacón will be your protector. And when Mauricio and Rosenda have found a place, then they will come back and get you. You are a pretty boy, Pepe. Father Chacón likes Pepe very much." The priest stood up and walked over to the far wall where he straightened one of the Cub Scout pictures. "Get some sleep, Pepe."

Rosenda came into the room. "Oh, Father Chacón, you're in here."

"Yes, Rosenda. Father Chacón was admiring your miracle."

"Isn't he beautiful?"

"He is that, my child. Beautiful."

Father Chacón's virtues have been excommunicated by the outside world; the most vital drives obscured by his depressive emotions, suspicion, fright, shame. The equation of moral decay. The equation for psychological devolution. Father

Chacón does furtively what he does best, loves and needs to do, with sustained anxiety that makes his heart weaken; and because of the danger, the threat of discovery and persecution, Father Chacón harvests a crop of animal instincts that cannot be tamed by the society that does not understand him. A gelded society, impotent spiritually, not comprehending the place of the body in God's perfect scheme, God's flawless method, the touch of a man of God, the touch of Father Chacón, the touch of Holiness, sweet Holiness. Father Chacón is no criminal. The boys . . . the boys . . .

supplement

Steimmel and Davis were on the run, enemies of the government, but they were not *public* fugitives. There were no news flashes of their images on television, no bulletins circulated through the ranks of local police agencies. Their arrest was supposed to have been the last anyone heard or thought of them. They were to be sneaked out of the nation's memory and consciousness by lack of coverage. Everyone had agreed. There was no baby to produce in evidence and to produce the baby in concept would have been to jeopardize national security. No one could know about Ralph and what Ralph could do or the fact there could even be a Ralph. Why, the mere possibility of a Ralph would terrify the nation. What if the commies had a Ralph or an Omar or a Vladi? And worse, what if some nuts out in the hinterlands took it upon themselves to challenge the morality of abusing a baby in the manner prescribed by good military thinking?

Somehow Steimmel and Davis understood all this and felt safe at least to the extent that the local cop on the beat was not after them, realizing all the while that the government agents could look like anyone on the street. The doctors panhandled enough money to buy food and some garments from a vintage-clothing store, then made their way south by hitchhiking. In Santa Monica, they appeared at the door of a screenwriter friend of Davis, an old boyfriend who had ended the relationship because of Ronald. In fact, when he let the women in, he said to Davis, "So, where's what his name?"

"I don't know and I don't care," Davis said.

"The two of you had a falling out? Did he walk out on you because you decided to descend another rung down the evolutionary ladder?"

Steimmel frowned, trying to catch up. "Hey, wait a second, you little pipsqueak."

Davis sought to calm Steimmel. "Don't listen to him. He's just trying to compensate for his little thingie and get to me through you."

"I am not standing in his way!" Steimmel pointed a finger at the man. "If you want to get to her, do it!"

"Steimmel, this is Melvin. Melvin, Steimmel." Davis walked across the room and looked out the window at the street. "We need a place to rest for a couple of days. And some money."

"Oh, of course," Melvin said. "I'll just go to sleep on the street, but first I'll go empty my bank account for you."

"You slept with him?" Steimmel asked Davis.

"Just twice."

"Get out," Melvin said.

"Melvin, I really need your help. The government is after us." Davis tried to look pathetic, biting her lip and hanging her head slightly.

"Whose government?"

"Our government. Why else would we be frightened?" Davis walked over and sat on the sofa, pushed through the magazines on the coffee table. There were no stories that were alarmingly new on the covers and no pictures of her or Steimmel or Ralph.

Steimmel went to the refrigerator and opened the door, stuck in her head, and came back with a beer in her hand.

"Help yourself," Melvin said. He walked over and sat by Davis on the sofa. "You can't stay here."

"Just for a couple of days, Melvin."

"No, no, no, no, no, no. I've got a new girlfriend."

"Good for you."

Steimmel fell into the chair across the coffee table from Davis and Melvin and took a swig of the beer. She stared at Melvin, unblinking.

Melvin was unnerved by Steimmel. He turned to Davis, "I don't want you here. I don't want Cynthia to find you here."

"Cynthia," Davis repeated the name. To Steimmel, she said, "Cynthia is her name." She said the name into the air. "I've always wanted to be a CYNthia. Tell me, Mel, is she hot?"

"Okay, that's it! Out!" When neither of the women moved, Melvin said, "If you're not out in three seconds, I'm calling the police."

That was when Steimmel produced the pistol and instructed Melvin to sit down and shut up.

anfractuous

Like all stories, any of these I offer here has another side.[4] My depiction of
the stories of my *life,* if you will, is not mere hedonistic practice, no mere
anarchism. Nor am I about a self-serving and uncomplex upbraiding of
any poststructuralist thinking, however bedazzled such thinking might be
by its own reflection, mesmerized and mechanically decisive in the face of
academic action. The *presence* of the stories at all betrays some other *reading.* All I can do is give my text a helmet and condoms and send it out into
the world. After Hiroshima, Auschwitz, and Blood River, there are no simple stories, there are no good neighborhoods, there are no safe meanings.
Meaning has become a spatial metaphor for presence, a kind of constant
self-pinching and asking if we're really awake. But if you pinch too hard,
you leave a bruise, a mark, a mark that might be construed as a gesture, and
any gesture is quite simply that, but it occupies space and so must have a
meaning and any meaning is just what we've said it is and oh, what a circle, what a circle, what a circle.

will the circle be unbroken?
by and by, lord, by and by

Father Chacón came back into the bedroom singing. "M-I-C, K-E-Y,
M-O-U-S-E." He stood at the foot of the bed and stared at me. I looked
at the closed door behind him. "Your new parents are sleeping in the shed
out back. I told them you would be warmer in here with me."

unties of simulacrum

Colonel Bill, after a short and disappointing fueling stop at Strategic Air
Command, flew his jet all over central and southern California hoping to
spot his baby. From twenty thousand feet he could, of course, see nothing,
and a couple of passes at fifteen hundred feet over the streets of Los Angeles
and Long Beach only made the people below look like ants (in fact, to his
thinking, they were ants), but he could not spot his baby. After several near

---

4. Here I defer to popular wisdom, however against my grain and better judgment, it
being the case that I, personally, do not adhere to the logical necessity of many or even
one extra interpretation or decoding of a given story. I constantly consider the literal
and come back with positive reports. It's not the simplicity of the literal, but the clean-
ness of it, the weight of it, and, lastly, the fact that nothing makes such a figurative comment on everything like a literal statement.

misses with commercial airliners and a traffic helicopter, Colonel Bill landed his craft at March Air Force Base. From there he drove his Hummer to a nearby Filipino doughnut shop in Moreno Valley, where he sat and ate an apple fritter and drank a cup of black coffee. He stared at each of the customers as they came in. He passed the time chatting with the owner whom he knew.

"I don't know where to start, Ferdinand, but it might as well be here," Colonel Bill said.

"What are you looking for?" Ferdinand said.

"Can't tell you."

"Secret, eh? I keep many secrets, both here and at my home in Manila. Did you know that I was once tried for murder?"

"Murder? No shit?"

"No shit," Ferdinand said. "They said I assassinated this guy. This guy was an enemy of my father. That was in nineteen thirty-three. But I wasn't tried until nineteen forty."

"Seven years? Were you in the pokey all that time?"

Ferdinand laughed. "No, no."

"So, you got off." Colonel Bill took a bite of fritter while he watched the man nod. "Did you do it?"

Ferdinand laughed. "I got off."

Colonel Bill laughed, too.

"I really miss the Philippines when I'm here." Ferdinand poured himself a cup of coffee and took a sip. "You know, there I'm considered a hero. I led the resistance against the Japanese back during World War Two, you know. I was in the Bataan Death March."

"Damn Nips."

Ferdinand nodded.

"You've seen a lot," Colonel Bill said. "Now you have this shop and a presidency."

"Yes, and two hundred thirty-seven million dollars. I love America."

The two men laughed together.

Melvin shook his head. "Let me get this straight," he said. "The two of you have twelve advanced degrees between you and all you could come up with was smashing the guy in the face with your skull?"

"It worked," Steimmel said.

"So, what are you going to do to me?" Melvin asked.

"I haven't decided. Just remember, *Mel,* we've got nothing to lose."

"I'll keep that in mind."

Davis was pacing the carpet in front of the window. "Steimmel, I'm stumped. I don't know how we're going to find that baby. The baby is the sign and I can't even find him in my meta-perceptual field." She began to sink. " And now I don't even have Ronald. He was a good subject. Made Washoe seem like a rodent."

Steimmel sneered. "That ape couldn't communicate. It was Clever Hans Phenomenon and you know it."

"It was not!" Davis shouted.

Melvin chuckled.

"What are you laughing at?" Davis asked.

"You two."

"Tell me, Melvin, what kind of movies do you write?" Steimmel asked, mockingly engaged.

"I write action movies."

Steimmel smiled and nodded. "I see. You write those phasic-level, mind-numbing, socially irredeemable, bar-dropping, celluloid anal wipettes. Well, I take photographs of ideas."

Davis snorted out a laugh. "Yeah, Melvin, you're Tavolga's plot man. How do we find one particular baby out amongst twenty million people?"

"First of all, from what you tell me, your baby's not out there among twenty million people. Some fantastic government agency has your baby. Some secret spy company has your baby in some covert day care."

"Shall I just shoot him now?" Steimmel asked Davis.

"He's right," Davis said. "They've probably got the little sucker tucked away in a missile silo somewhere."

"You two can leave anytime," Melvin said. "I won't call the police. I promise. Just walk out and I'll say I never saw you. Please."

"Stop begging, Melvin," Davis snapped. "That's why I left you. Always begging. Begging for sex. Then begging for me to stop."

"I left you, monkey-slut," Melvin said.

"Keep dreaming," Davis said.

"Okay, that's it!" Melvin said, standing. "Both of you, out of my fucking house, right now!"

Steimmel and Davis looked at each other and laughed.

bridge

GOD: Roland, do you think it was a good idea to go put your penis in that young graduate student's vagina and move it around?

BARTHES: It had to be done. My penis is an extension, not of myself, but of the the very signification of my meaning, of my marks on any page, whether made by me when writing or arbitrarily marking. I'm French, you know.

GOD: It's just that Douglas was so counting on her continued admiration.

BARTHES: I can't help that. If my penis hadn't been in her, where would it have been? If not there, where? My penis, the instrument you gave me, the extension finally of you, of you and the other two sides of the triangle. Pulchritude.

GOD: And you did make a pass at his wife, however unsuccessful.

BARTHES: She's crazy, that one. Neither of them are French, you know.

exousai

As I recall Michelangelo's god reaching down from above to touch the hand of Adam in whatever sacramental action is meant to represent, am I to be moved in a way that my more *obscure* rendering of the same *touching* cannot achieve because of my lack of literal *artistic* vision? The colors and line and form, even mere size, might well impress, but to move from that appreciation of craft to a spiritually moving encounter, regardless of my cultural connectedness and proximity to the work itself is not a compelling notion to a baby unmoved by talk of heaven and the garden and the devil. After all, my conception of a god is perhaps more to be trusted, as I am closer to that thing than any other *gesturing* being, my not having been corrupted by indoctrination and poorly told Biblical tales, and being a more recent arrival from the big house. And so, one might tell me that because of the "power of art" that chapel ceiling does more to achieve its end than say Schnabel in his amorphous blue depiction of the Almighty. But I come back to my image. The baby on the bed being approached by the fat priest, two pictures of Norwegian cub scouts adorning the wall behind him while the parents of the youth are tucked away in some cold room far away from the fray.

As the good father approached, I found it in myself to grab paper and pencil from the nightstand beside me and scribble,

I do not understand the nature of your approach. I am young and naive, but be warned that I am capable of accurate and detailed representation of any turn of events.

I handed the note to the stunned man. He fell to his knees in the middle of the room and broke into an immediate sweat across his brow, his prayer requiring, apparently, much exertion, his lips working madly and forming unintelligible words. Then he opened his eyes and stared at me, backed away, his face full of fear. "My Lord," he said. "My Lord." He turned and snatched the crucifix from the wall and held it to face me. He was shocked and terrified by the fact that the symbol caused me no discernible discomfort or consternation. He found the knob of the door behind him and backed out, closing me in, leaving me alone.

ens realissimum

To wonder whether any age has failed is, of course, to miss the point. Snipers on the high ridge of the twentieth century can pick off the artists as they come out for food, but the work has not miscarried or failed. No more than dinosaurs were blunders of nature, no more than a fully conversant baby is a sign from god or the devil. Why make art? Why the gesture at all? Why worry? Let them all graze. Let the glaciers come. But, of course, my meaning is solely that, no more, simply what it is, sarcastic as it might be, a housel of sorts for the irreligious, an anthem for enemies of the state, a prayer to the dead god Plato. Things don't twist, things don't change, things don't stay the same, things don't *do* anything.

The Period Is the Point

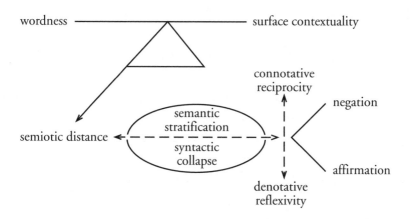

RALPH

G

différance

Staring at the door that had just been closed by the priest, I wondered if there was no inside and outside to the spirit of being, no body and soul, no opposite side to any orientation, but that we were Möbius surfaces, our topologies defined by the fact that we can never get around them to the other side, but are always there, both on the other side and staring at it confusedly, longingly, with much apprehension and eagerness. And if in an egomaniacal fit of reason I extrapolate from my picture of the individual to the world, perhaps the case is that there is no distinction between the real world and that which constitutes real for us in the use of this thing called language. There is no split or rupture from the world when it comes to the reporting of the *real,* as the consciousness of it is on the same side of the paradoxical tape, the Möbius strip of the world, all in the same place, tucked away in the same box in the attic, living in the same cage at the zoo. In fact, all fantasy, desire, falsehood, and delusion exist together with the *real* and language and so are all the same, which is why adults are prone to the supposedly irrational utterance, "This isn't happening," when under duress, but of course by even saying it isn't happening, it is made so. Since there is, as I have said, no digression, let me add: The accused cannot deny guilt, for to deny it is to recognize it and so it is when denying the act itself, but to deny understanding of the charge is to deny the language, the soup in which the action and the guilt and the falsehood and the fantasy are all stirred. Such denial might well serve not only to get one off the hook but to erase the crime of which one is guilty anyway. Such was the case with the priest. Under his bed I found a scrapbook with newspaper clippings about his alleged activities with young boys in his last parish. He looked younger in one photograph, but by the clipping's date I knew it was not so long ago. All along the margins were scribbled questions, all of a kind, asking more or less, "What does this mean?" or "I can't even imagine what they're describing." The questions were interesting to me, because, as is the custom with newspapers, the stories of what reportedly transpired were so sketchy that I had no idea what had supposedly happened. The strangest thing was that the man had actually saved the clippings. Whether a sign of guilt or innocence, I do not know, but there they were, neatly pasted and taped onto the thick manila pages.

I resolved, as you can well guess, not to be there when Father Friendly returned. I went to the closet, the door of which was ajar, thinking that I would hide in there and then upon being found missing[1] I would exit via the door of the bedroom. But as it turned out, inside the closet was a small door. I opened it and stepped through it into a corridor in which I could barely stand. I followed it.

subjective-collective

One Physicist to another: I hate your GUT.

MERLEAU-PONTY: Imagine you're looking at a big arrow.

LACAN: Consider it imagined. Are you now going to ask me which way it's pointing?

MERLEAU-PONTY: No. You're seeing it. Now, imagine that it is invisible.

LACAN: Done.

MERLEAU-PONTY: Which way is it pointing?

LACAN: To the left.

MERLEAU-PONTY: Are you still imagining it?

LACAN: Yes.

---

1. An interesting expression that drives home my theory, but, as I have shaped my theory, even to negate it would have it be true. *Missing Meaning Turns Up Found,* the headline reads. Or perhaps, *Meaning Found to Be Missing.*

incision

a

We do here
what we do
in a host of familiar cases.
Ask about relations,
about the thing named.
Recall the picture
of that thing.
Tell me which way it points.
Tell me its color.
And whether it can
be broken into pieces.
A queer conception,
sublime logic.

b

Let us assume X.
Even such signs have
some place, some
language X.
Constituent parts
compose this reality—
molecules, atoms, simple
X.

c

From rags and dust
a rat is formed in the cellar.
It was not there before.
Only rags and dust.

exousai

I walked through that channel like the rat in the maze that Steimmel would have had me be. It was dark in there and there were many webs, but a tiny light at the end of it pulled me forward. I came to the end and saw that the light was from a room on the other side of a peephole. The room was furnished with stiff and square chairs and somber colors, brown and maroon. Father Chacón was waving his arms and talking to Mauricio and Rosenda, running his stubby fingers through the hair about his ears, then slamming his fat hands together as if in prayer.

"The child is possessed!" the priest said. "The devil is in him as certainly as I am standing here before you!" He held his face up to the dim light of the ornate chandelier.

Rosenda began to weep loudly and Mauricio held her. "It cannot be true," she said. "He's such a beautiful baby. He's a good boy."

"No, no, no. He is the devil's tool! He wrote a note. The devil controlled his hand and he wrote a note."

Rosenda pleaded with Mauricio. "Please, go get little Pepe so that Father Chacón can see how sweet he is."

"He wrote letters on paper," the priest said.

Mauricio left to collect me.

"Please, God," Rosenda prayed out loud. "Please let the Father know how good my child is. Tell him that Pepe is not possessed,"

"Say what you will, Rosenda, but it will not change the truth. We must have an exorcism at once."

Mauricio came running back, out of breath. He said, "The child, he is gone. He wasn't in the room. I couldn't find him."

"The devil is loose in the house of God!" Father Chacón wailed. "Lord, protect us!"

seme

> "Killed she was, with an illocutionary ax."
> "She didn't have a chance, I heard."
> "Done as soon as said, it was."
> "Say it isn't so."

Of the man who so loved metaphor, it was said that he wore a simile from ear to ear upon reading the first pages of Joyce's *Finnegans Wake.* He was said to be counting the *dasein* until the book came out. But when he awoke the morning of the publication date, he learned that all metaphors had gone on strike, saying collectively that they were underpaid and miserably misunderstood by their employers. What their demands were remained unclear even after a second news conference.

> *Hath Romeo slain himself? Say thou but* I,
> *And that bare vowel* I *shall poison more*
> *Then the death darting eye of Cockatrice,*
> I *am not* I, *if there be such an* I.
> *Or those* eyes *shut, that makes thee answer* I.
> *If he be slain say* I; *or if not, no.*
>
> (*Romeo and Juliet,* III. ii)

Of the letter *I*, I have nothing to say, except where would I be without it and that there is no situation more self-affirming as seeing I to I with one-self. And there is no mutiny as when I can't believe my *I's,* as when one is accutely harassed and appears to be the *I* of the needled.

anfractuous

Steimmel and Davis ordered pizza and had it delivered to Melvin's apartment, tipping the cute Indian boy generously and then laughing about his turban once the door was closed. "Thank you very much for the incredibly handsome tip, madam," Davis mocked the rapid accent of the kid. "Who talks like that?"

Steimmel put the pizza on the counter and peeked into the box. "I never thought I'd look at a pizza the way I am now," she said.

"How's that?" Davis asked.

"As food."

Melvin tried to say something, but the pair of his briefs stuffed into his mouth made his sounds unintelligible. His wrists were bound with a neck-tie behind his back and to the stiff-backed chair in which he sat in the center of the living room. Davis looked at him as she tried to take a bite of pizza, pulling it away from her lips because it was too hot.

"Shit," she said. "Now, I'm going to have those little pieces of skin hanging from the roof of my mouth." She walked over and stood in front of Melvin. "What do you think, Steimmel? Should we let Mel eat?"

"He can have what's left," Steimmel said.

"Okay." Davis went to the refrigerator and grabbed a beer, opened it, and leaned back against the counter. "I feel sick," she said. "Not physically sick, but lost. I don't know where I am or where I'm going. I've always known exactly where I was going. I knew where I was going to college and graduate school and where I was going to do my postdoc and even where I was going to publish my first article and my first book and I knew it all when I was only twelve. And now, I don't know where I'm going to sleep tomorrow night. Direction has always been a kind of neurosis for me and to have it taken away, well, it's shattering. But also freeing. Do you know what I mean?"

Steimmel nodded with a mouth full of cheese and pepperoni, then said around her food, "I was the same kind of obsessional neurotic. In fact, I had dreams, rather nightmares, when I was a child that my mother and father were forcing my future into my anus like suppositories." She caught Davis's expression and continued, "I know, I know. But the enema wasn't the half of it. In the dream, I would defecate myself out as a doctor or a great scholar and my parents would praise me wildly while wiping the shit from me."

Melvin managed to spit out his underwear and he screamed at the top of his lungs, "You're both fucking lunatics!"

The two women studied him briefly and then broke into hysterical laughter. "You don't know the half of it, Melvin," Steimmel said. She pulled a chair over and sat beside him, put her lips close to his chubby cheek and said, "You see it wasn't just getting out what you put in that my parents were achieving in my dream. It was a kind of treatment for my deeper problem, my self-clogging, so to speak. The whole idea was a kind of glycerinic signifier for washing out whatever impaction was so crippling me. Perhaps that's why I became an *anal*-yst."

"Would you please shoot me now?"

donne lieu

The water that is spirit, the water of all things, the water of tears, the water of blood, dream water, streams, and rivers where life begins, where things are washed, like Circe in that creek, the dreams like water, mixing with water, like water, the water that is a kiss, water, that drink, full of parasites, drink it only when it flows faster than you can walk.

But here am I, young Ralph, hidden away in the walls of a house of some god, watching through peepholes while priests sprinkle holy water in the corners and toss nervous glances to each other.

"Father Chacón," a tall priest called. "How will we recognize the baby in question?"

"Why, Father O'Blige," said Chacón with mock patience, "he is the only baby here. If you see a baby, then it's the right baby, it's the devil. And do not assume that the devil has not the power to change the appearance of this child."

"How big is the baby?" asked Father O'Blige.

"I don't know. Baby-size."

"I'd hate to splash holy water on the wrong baby."

Father Chacón rubbed a palm over his face. "If, for the sake of argument, there is another baby running around here and that second baby is not the devil, then what ill effects will the holy water have if administered to him?"

"None, I suppose."

"Very good. Now, keep searching! And keep praying and splashing the water around. The devil will be burned by the spirit of God and the baby will come out into the open. Then we will drive Lucifer from the little body and back into the deep recesses of hell!"

Rosenda was now dressed in a black dress and was wearing a larger cross around her neck, being attended to by a pair of hefty, black-wrapped nuns whose fingers were busy with rosaries. Rosenda kept wailing my name, my name as far as she was concerned, and effectively my name as when she wailed it, I knew that she was referring to me. Steimmel might have seen a thousand "little bastards" in her lifetime, but Rosenda had seen only one Pepe and if O'Blige's second baby had crawled in at that moment and caused Rosenda to say, "Pepe," I would have thought, *Impostor!* So, I was Ralph, the little bastard who also went by Pepe.

Mauricio was seated on a bench against the far wall. He was alone and his expression was more or less unchanged. He looked a little weary, but he always looked weary. He watched closely as the bearded priest who stood near him crossed himself repeatedly.

"You should be praying, my son," the priest said to Mauricio. "You should be praying for your salvation."

Mauricio nodded. The priest splashed him with some of the special juice and blessed him. Mauricio nodded again and closed his eyes.

unties of simulacrum

Fragments are perhaps woven like threads, but maybe even driven like spikes into tracks, and serve to create the thing itself, and in so doing, the thing itself increasingly magnetizes; thus it constructs itself, without mission, without sense of parts, but only of the whole, an endeavor both finite and perpetual like the business of language itself. To call any portion of any language or life or story a fragment is to miss the point or at least to beg the question. In fact, there are no fragments, but each part of language, life, or story are, in the spirit of Leibniz's monads, whole, complete, and self-contained. There is no more space between what we routinely and naively refer to as a fragment and its presumed parent whole than there is between me and my name. My arm is a fragment only if I am blown to bits and even then, if I come around to your house looking for my appendage, you will not say, "I have your fragment in the kitchen on ice." To understand a piece is to understand a whole. *Understanding* as a thing must be the same whether understanding an algebra problem or why the sky is blue, the only difference being the stuff understood. *I understood something once and it felt just like this.* And so if you tie this to the whole and recognize it as the anti-fragment that it is, and do not consider it a piece of the thing it purports to have nothing to do with, it existing from page whatever to page whatever, then you must understand that this is finally no anti-fragment either, because the whole thing argues against the thing itself and its negation. What a circle. The tangle of an intransitive verb. Infinite verb has no home. Finite verbs run in packs like feral dogs.

derivative

Colonel Bill drove while Ferdinand leaned out through the passenger-side window, whistling and calling to women on the street. "Hey, baby!" he shouted. "Want a pair of Joan and David slingbacks with three-inch heels?!" The women ignored him and he fell back into the seat, stared ahead through the windshield. "I'm really homesick."

"I was in the Philippines once. Killed a bunch of people and left."

"Me, too. At least the killing part." Marcos looked out at a new group of women, but didn't call to them. "So, you going to tell me what you're looking for? You know, I've got ears on the street. I have to keep up with what the people are up to."

"I'm looking for a baby," Colonel Bill said.

"A baby?"

"A very special baby. A brown baby. That's all I can tell you."

"A baby. Imagine that." Marcos opened a chrome flask and took a swig. "Want some?"

Colonel Bill shook his head.

"Did you know that my wife has over three thousand pairs of shoes?" Marcos took another drink from his flask.

"I'd heard something like that."

"Those shoes are a problem. Everybody knows about her shoes. 'You've only got two feet,' I said to her. I said, 'What do you need all those shoes for?' Know what she said?"

"What'd she say?"

"She told me to shut up before she put on some Gucci boots and kicked my ass."

ennuyeux

I wondered while hiding there in the hallowed walls of god's house whether tigers knew they were striped cats, whether mules found each other stubborn, whether language ever lacked meaning. I wondered whether meanings were the stripes on words and marveled at how words always erased themselves but never disappeared. I wondered where the window of meaning opened and what was in its place before, nonmeaning? nonsense? nondisjunction?[2] nonfeasance? The baby was bored in the back room.

The new morning was pushing light through the gaudy stained windows in the big room where now all of the team of priests had gathered. Mauricio and Rosenda sat on the far bench with the nuns. The priests were about to launch into some kind of cleansing ceremony when there was a knock at the door.

When Father Chacón opened the door a couple of men stepped in along with one woman. The men wore caps which read KIDD. The woman wore a bright red dress, her hair hanging loosely in the most controlled way imaginable. The men carried large cases and rolls of cable. The woman carried nothing. The woman said, "I'm Jenny Jenson from KIDD, I hope you haven't forgotten what today is." Her tone was friendly on the verge of joking.

"Today?" Father Chacón said.

"My god," Jenny Jenson said, "you have forgotten." She gave a glance at her crew, then looked back at the priest. "It's that day of the year, Father. It's the day that the mission's bearded irises open."

---

2. But instead of chromosomes, we perhaps have signifier and signified failing to separate subsequent to meaning in metaphor or metonymy, so that one, signifier or signified, has both meaning and misunderstanding and the other has nothing.

"Oh, yes," Father Chacón said. "We'll be right out."

"We'll be setting up," Jenny Jenson said. "And hurry please, the light is good now, but it looks like it wants to get cloudy out here."

"We'll be out directly," Chacón said and pushed the door shut.

I was able to hear Jenny Jenson say just before the door was closed, "He actually forgot, for crying out loud."

Father Chacón turned and leaned his back against the door. "This is awful. It's the Opening of the Irises and I forgot all about it. It's that devil." He shook his head and looked at the other priests. "First things first. We've got to get that news crew on its way. So, we're going to go out there and bless those fucking flowers and get those people the hell back in here."

The nuns gasped.

"Sorry, sisters," Chacón said. "Okay. Are you ready, O'Blige? O'Boie? O'Meye?"

The other priests nodded.

"All right, then. Everybody outside. No one is safe in here alone." Chacón gave a look at the walls, his gaze passing over me. I watched them file out into the light of the day. I went back along the corridor, opened the little door, and came out through the closet into the priest's room, which was now disheveled from having been searched.

libidinal economy

Mo's friend Clyde, because she asked him to, put his penis in her vagina and moved it around. It was, in fact, my mother's vagina, but I had no fond recollections of it and I certainly had no stake in what or whom she chose to put into it. I assume that there was some beneficial result, though I had witnessed the contrary when she had done the same with my father. She requested it and did it because she wanted to feel tenderness, something my father had long been unable to offer. And sadly, even when present, I was also incapable of much softness. I resigned myself to thinking the deficiency was a function of my overdeveloped intellect, though I did not believe that such was logically necessary, but only sufficient and I denied any notion that my hardness was an inherited character trait. Afterward, Mo hugged the man tightly, but she didn't whisper anything to him, but she just squeezed him and prayed that I was okay.

My mother was not a believer in any god, but I knew that wherever she was, she was praying for my welfare and safe delivery. I wondered if by praying she was indeed creating god, making god real, and if real for her, then real for everyone, real, as a god, supposedly by definition, should and must be. I had no tobacco can to toss high into the air before shouting, "The ontological argument is sound," but I did know that my intense desire to see a unicorn was not manufacturing a herd anywhere. And I wondered how god worked as metaphor, the concept of god being like *God,* the absolute Other, infinity and irreducible alterity. I considered my mother like god in a way, not as life-giving, but as one in a set of parentheses, left or right, yielding either the promise of sense coming or of sense rendered, the negation of spatial exteriority within language itself. I had nostalgic feelings about my mother's attempt to connect me to her own postulates of sense in the world, regardless of the absence of obvious meaning in language, despite the general lack of connectedness in her own personal experience. I remembered once when I was just days old, she confided in me and told me, more or less, that life was empty and meaningless. She said, "I'm sorry." In her painting, especially after my departure she was attempting to construct an anatomy of grief, not for my loss, but for hers.

In the morning, Mo asked Clyde to leave. She wasn't angry with him. She wasn't annoyed with him. She wasn't uncomfortable. She wasn't in love with him. She was glad they'd had sex. He had been what my father had never been, there to express affection rather than prowess, but still it was no answer to any question that plagued her.

spacing

BARTHES: Nonetheless, it is questionable whether my account of our sexual encounter will coincide with your depiction, the form itself being compromising at best and perhaps by nature. Discontinuity, instability, and dissatisfaction cannot evade wresting their meaning from the orbits of continuity, stability, and satisfaction. So, there you have it, an invitation to sublate, to integrate, to seek out the limits of conceptual thought and logical identity and the comprehensive destruction of reason. Are you certain you didn't have an orgasm?

LAURA: Yes.

bridge

Tunica Vaginalis

While I still resembled
a fish,
the pouch
dropped from my stomach
into my scrotum.

By a distinct crease
it connects the testis
with the epididymus,
the inner surface free

smooth,
covered by a layer,
tissue of the heart,
the upper portion
long since obliterated,

though it may be seen
as a fibrous thread
lying loose
in the areolar tissue
around my cord.

ootheca

Zing!
"Well, I think the interview went just fine, Professor Townsend."
"That call is for me, I guess. They're boarding my section now."
"It was really nice meeting you."
"So, you think I might be hearing from you in the next week or so?"
"Oh, yeah, right. You don't want to miss your plane."

ens realissimum

I made my way through the empty building to the very front door through which the team of holy men and the others had exited. The door was ajar and through the crack of it I could see them all there in the garden. Purple and lavender, yellow and white bearded irises standing nearly as tall as Rosenda, in huge mobs of color. A Morning Cloak butterfly flitted about blanket flowers, poppies, and cosmos beyond them in the garden.

The priests were whispering in a huddle, Father Chacón in the center, while the film crew and reporter set up the last of their equipment. Mauricio put his arm over Rosenda's shoulder and pulled her well off to the side, behind an exhibit of some kind of grain grinder, away from the cameras, away from detection by the outside world. Rosenda was lost, her eyes empty, her short-fingered, fleshy hands limp and useless by her sides.

ephexis

As a narrator telling my tale and not someone else's tale, can I arrest the illusion of the tale being a fiction? But since you have come to this under the pretense of the work being a fiction, the book being so classified, then even I am an illusion. I am in exile from my own fiction, which turns out to be my reality, for I may insist on the truth of the telling only if I acknowledge it as fiction. It is perhaps a kind of figurative displacement or a resignation to a kind of self-reflexive, gesturing untruth, which is neither lie nor truth, but functions as an anaphoric hermeneutic.[3] Derr we have it.

I offer no information about society. I offer no truth about the culture. I offer only however many words there are here in the text and the frequency and order in which they are written, along with the marks ruling their starting, stopping, and pausing. I do not love humankind. Humankind does not love me. And though I answer to a couple of names and several descriptions, there is only one name that answers to me.

To make a liar of myself, let me offer just one truth: The search for the origins of reason, logic, and thinking is as sensible as the search for the origins of the bodily function called defecation.

---

3. Although any talk of a "hermeneutic reading" seems to belabor the obvious, to wave tattered, tautological flags of the understanding of meaning.

causa sui

From the doorway in which I stood I could see across the courtyard to another building, the door of which was wide open. To get there I would have to pass behind the irises and the ceremony, but there was the promise of cover from a hedge of gardenias. I squeezed through the door and stepped as quickly as I could to hide behind a large terra-cotta pot. I then made a dash for the hedge. The smell of of the blooms was intoxicating. I made my way slowly, hearing the voices of the priests as they offered a prayer of thanks for the irises. Then Jenny Jenson was putting questions to Father Chacón. I came to a gap in the hedge that I had been unable to see from the doorway. I glanced around the bush at the black backs of the priests. I tried to sprint across the opening, but I tripped and fell, face first into the dirt. The priests didn't turn around, but I felt the eye of the camera seek me out and define me.

"Do the irises bloom on the same day every year?" Jenny Jenson asked the priest.

Chacón nodded. "Yes, Jenny. Our bearded irises seem to have a rather precise clock. Regardless of the weather or the amount of rainfall, our irises open this day, every year, like clockwork. We see it as testimony to God's eternal precision."

"Do you do anything special to keep them so lovely? Fertilizer, that sort of thing?"

"We weed and water, but the loveliness? That has nothing to do with any action of ours. And no, we don't fertilize."

"Do you spray for insects?"

"Well, yes, we do that regularly."

Steimmel put another chopsticks load of fried rice into her mouth, then pointed at the television screen. "Would you look at that fat bastard. Like hell he doesn't fertilize those plants."

Davis sat beside her on the sofa and picked up the carton of sweet and sour chicken. "I hate priests," she said. "My parents tried to raise me to be a Catholic. I could never understand that. They weren't even Catholic. They said they thought the structure would be good for me."

As the doctors watched the screen, the camera zoomed in on a small form pulling itself from the dirt.

"Hey, that's our baby!" Steimmel shouted.

Colonel Bill and Ferdinand were standing in Big Carl's Electronics Warehouse in Moreno Valley. Big Carl was showing Ferdinand an impossibly large, portable cassette-playing machine with detachable speakers.

"This thing gets so loud you wouldn't believe," Big Carl said. "It even scares me. Say you want to drive somebody out of a building they're holed up in. Well, you put a tape of some of that rock 'n' roll music in this baby and set up the speakers and crank it up and they'll be out soon enough. I guarantee it."

Marcos ran his finger across the black plastic. "What other colors does it come in? You know, of course, I can buy this for a quarter of the price when I get back to Manila."

Colonel Bill had turned away from the sales pitch and was watching a twenty-nine-inch RCA Victor color television. The camera zoomed past a fat priest standing in front of some flowers to a small form pulling itself from the dirt.

"That's my fucking baby!" Colonel Bill shouted.

Eve had just settled in at the kitchen table with a cup of tea and the newspaper. She glanced up at the television on the counter.

"My baby. My Ralph."

supernumber

THALES: I don't have time for you today.

BRUNEAU: You don't have time anyway. Time is not something one can have. Etic, emic, or otherwise.

THALES: You've been hanging out with that Hall again. I don't have time for him either. You'd stroll in here and have me believe that time is one-dimensional. Well, let me tell you, you and Leibniz and all who follow, time is not relative. Time is absolute. Lay it out on a line and there it is. You might even go back in it, but I'll point to the line and say, "How long did it take you to get there?" You might stop it, but I'll point to the line and say, "How long was it stopped?"

BRUNEAU: You're tired. You should rest.

THALES: Bullshit. You mean I'm old.

BRUNEAU: Would you like some water?

THALES: Very funny.

gesture
gaze
genesis
grouping
gyve

degrees

Mo was leaving the house when Roland Barthes stopped her.

"I've just seen my child on television," Eve said. "I've got to go get him." Her voice was shaking.

"You're in no condition to drive," said Barthes. "I'll ride with you."

Eve drove the old Saab as fast as it would go down the Pacific Coast Highway.

Steimmel drove while Davis read the map. They were in Melvin's yellow BMW 2002, rolling down Interstate 405.

Colonel Bill's Hummer was humming along down I-215 to I-15. Ferdinand sang along with Aretha Franklin.

I was now in the the chapel of the mission, a scary cavern of gaudiness and mawkishness. The only thing understated was subtlety. I crawled down the thin red carpet of an outer aisle toward the altar. I heard the faint sound of the kind of muttering I had come to associate with prayer. As I approached the shining, gilded mess of gold and stained glass, I wondered if any kind of appreciation of the spiritual might come over me. But all I could think was, wow, I bet this cost a bundle. There were golden birds and golden angels, which looked a little like me, on the walls. The place was lighted to best effect, I suppose, but I found it hard to believe that so much gold needed help from decisively placed spots. Tall candles stood unlit.

I made my way through a doorway to the left of the altar and sat in a corner of a room that seemed relatively unused. There were cobwebs all about and a layer of dust was undisturbed on the table and chairs.

"See, I told you I saw a baby," a man's voice said.

I must have been lost in thought or perhaps even asleep, because I hadn't heard anyone come in. The voice belonged to one of the camera crew and he was walking toward me. I got up and tried to run, but the man scooped me up.

"I'm not going to hurt you, little fellow," he said. He was hairy with big hands and he smelled of some kind of food.

Jenny Jenson was close behind him. "So, it's a baby. Big deal."

"So," the man said to me. "Who do you belong to?" He bounced me on his arm as if that would improve my mood.

The fat Father Chacón then came into the room. "You've found him!" he said. "Thank the Lord!"

"Whose baby is this?" the cameraman asked.

"He's the devil's baby," the priest said. The other priests were now behind him in the doorway.

The man who held me laughed. "What are you talking about? He's just a little boy."

"We have to exorcise him!" Chacón shouted more forcefully than he seemed to intend. "He's possessed."

I put on the sweetest, most innocent face I could muster and the cameraman refused to give me up. He said, "I'm not giving this child to you. You're crazy. Where'd he come from? Tell me, where is the child's mother?" He took a step as if to get by the priests.

"I must have that baby!" Chacón said.

"No," said the cameraman.

"Get him!" Chacón shouted.

The cameraman dodged O'Blige and managed to kick O'Boie to the side. Jenny Jenson stood in Chacón's way and the cameraman pushed by O'Meye. Soon, we were outside the room and the clerics were inside. Chacón shouted for the others to "stop the heathens and get the devil-baby back!"

Jenny Jenson led the way up the center aisle of the chapel, the cameraman who held me close on her heels. The other members of the crew were standing at the door to the outside looking confused and lost. The priests sprinted up the aisles to the left and right of us. Father O'Blige came from the left and threw a body tackle into the cameraman. I flew from his arms and rolled forward onto the legs of Jenny Jenson, causing her to lose her balance, stumble, and fall.

"Don't let them get that baby!" the cameraman shouted to his crew.

The crew put down anything they were holding and a huge fight began. Priests threw punches and Jenny Jenson's nose was bloodied. Chacón was thrown by the soundman through some thin wooden doors. O'Meye tried to hurt a man with holy water, but was clocked with a right.

I rolled away from the fray, out the double doors, and into some bushes. From there I could see Mauricio and Rosenda looking on, puzzled, but unwilling to approach the excitement.

Are Meanings in the Head?

(Ralph's Theory of Fictive Space)
An appendix within the text for the purpose of serving the last sentence

A) What is is what is and all that is is all there is.

A.A) All that is is and the things therein are all there is therein, in the world, the world itself, fictive space.

A.AA) The world is what it is, the things therein having existence only so far as perception allows their being.

A.AB) All that is determines plot and characterization and all that will not happen as well, what is said, what is not said, what cannot be said.

A.AC) The world is what happens and the fiction is what is and only what is, not what has happened, but what must happen.

A.B) The world divides into chapters, and all that is divided also factors and so the world, the fiction, is fecund and at once final, dying without consequence.

A.BA) Each word that is the world lives in each space of logic with separate life and so, meaning; therefore meaning nothing beyond its place.

B._A) Story is not fiction, but a state of affairs that occupies fictive space, the logic therein being its own logic and true only to itself.

B._AA) The essentiality of events of the story, the actions, the reactions and pre-actions of fictive space are pieces of the world and each, at every turn, whole unto itself, identical to every other piece and the whole.

B._AB) In fictive space, no event is without inferential import, no event yields meaning arbitrarily, no event appears without breaking a twig or disappears without a trail.

B._ABA) No event exists untethered in fictive space, but any event may have tethered to it, accidentally or not, metaphoric or metonymic import that may itself finally exist untethered in the space of the fiction.

Though logical rules of actual space need not apply in the fiction, the logic of the fictive space is incorruptible and therefore, whereas in a fiction there can indeed be P &~P, there is less that is actually possible and probable than in real space.

B._ABB) It is not true that simply because a thing can be imagined as a part of a state of affairs with other things that that thing can necessarily be imagined outside any state of affairs or the possibility of such combinations with other things.

B._ABC) If Joseph loves Mary, then must I also know what it would be for Joseph to love Maggie or Damara or Ruth? If I know what this love is, then must I know it in all its possible combinations within the world? Or with Joseph alone? Yes. But I cannot know the thing, love, as a thing unto itself, without relation to Joseph with Mary, Damara, or Ruth or to Joseph alone.

B._ABCA) If I am to know what this thing, love, is then I must know that it cannot exist without a lover and a loved, that it has no internal properties without its association, that it is nothing without combinations and associations.

B._ABD) If all love is understood, then all lovers and all loved objects must be understood, all combinations and permutations of associative relations.

B._AC) Each word is complete within the fictive space it occupies. I can erase the word, but the space is there regardless. However, the space is always filled; even when empty, the space is not empty.

B._ACA) A word must be located in relation to other words in fictive space. Fictive space has no bounds, but it is inwardly infinite.

A sound in the fiction may not be a word, but is a *word* necessarily, a unit of the fictive material, meaning what the fiction requires of it.

Whatever properties the real world assigns a word untethered in real space mean nothing in fictive space.

B._AD) Words contain the possibility of infinite meaning, together or alone, in or outside of the fictive space.

B._ADA) Every word weighs what every other word weighs. Context is absolute authority.

B._B) Every word is simple, a simple unit, completely without meaning.

B._B_A) Every *use* of a word has a direct influence on the word itself and the meaning, and an indirect influence on the reception and interpretation of the meaning, but not the *use*.

B._BA) Sentences, though constructed of words, cannot be composites, but are the constituent and most simple components of the fiction. Sentences, however, are not the substance of the fiction or the fictive space.

B._BAA) If the fiction had no substance, then the *truth* of it would depend on the veracity of the sentences and so, would be dependent on the sentences having spatial location or orientation outside fictive space.

B._BAB) If such were true, then fictive space could not be drawn true to its own inherent logic.

B._BB) Fictive space must share some property or quality (though a quality cannot exist as a thing without a home) or form with actual space, that it might be understood as a world. But if there are no living things that move or communicate and no physical laws or negations of those laws to govern the behavior of bodies, animate and inanimate, then is fictive space suddenly collapsed?

B._BC) Is only one *real* thing necessary to make fictive space imaginable? A chair? Anger? Or is the word, or the sentence, that transcendent tie, the only *thing* required to validate the space?

B._BCA) Material properties of the fictive space do not require an appeal to actual space. The substance of the fiction is dependent on the tie to the real world, but has no constituent parts that are necessarily identical to anything *real*.

B._BCB) Simply speaking, words are just words, sentences are just sentences, meaning is nearly everything and nothing is as it seems.

B._BCC) If two worlds, different fictive spaces or a fictive space and actual space, have the same logic, then the only distinction between them is that they are different.

B._BCCA) A thing that occupies a position in fictive space cannot rely on the uniqueness and singularity of its spatial position as an essential distinguishing feature, as fictive space need not adhere to the laws of actual space.

B._BD) Story is what subsists autonomously, self-sufficiently, and independently of the form, logic, or any quality of the fictive space that contains and defines it.

B._BE) Story is story.

B._BEA) Particular character, plot, tone, voice, and time are bound to story within a particular fictive space.

B._BF) There must be character, plot, tone, voice, and time if fictive space can support story and so create an unalterable world.

B._BG) Particular story subsisting in various fictive spaces is at once, selfsame, identical, and different.

B._BGA) The conception of character, plot, tone, voice, and time (storiemes) is contingent not of conception, but on complete understanding and acceptance of the fictive space and the story.

B._BGB) Storiemes produce the fictive space.

B._C) In the story, the storiemes are the connective tissue, the ligaments and cartilage, but also the skeleton and musculature of the fictive space, but the story does not depend on storiemes.

B._CA) Storiemes are inextricably bound to each other for substance and fictive mission. Meaning is bound to story, but is subject to alteration by the occupation of different fictive spaces and configuration of storiemes.

B._CB) Storiemes are not self-generating.

B._CC) Logic is the possibility of story.

B._CD) The structure of the story follows from the possibility of the form and the inward focus of the storiemes.

B._D) The world is all that is possible within a particular fictive space.

B._E) Story is self-determining and therefore conceptually finite, but fictive space has no boundaries and only boundaries.

B._F) The world, story and, by extension, fictive space make up reality.

B._FA) Realities are dependent on fictive space.

B._FB) Fictive space contains, controls, and contributes truth in reality.

B.A) A story cannot be seen at once.

B.AA) A story exists in logical space, fictive space, real time and imagined.

B.AB) A story is a likeness of a world.

B.AC) In a story, storiemes represent corresponding and noncorresponding conceptions, objects, and subjects of a world within fictive space, and become reality.

B.ACA) In a story the constituent parts depend on the representational import of a world.

B.AD) What constitutes a story is that the parts, the storiemes, are not only associated in function and sense, but in necessary logical movement.

B.ADA) A story is a world.

B.AE) The fact that the constituent parts of a story are related and associated in ways paralleling a given world represent like relations and associations in reality.
This is the structure of a story.
The possibility of this structure is the form.

B.AEA) Story form is the possibility that the story represents a world.

B.AEAA) So, the story is attached to reality. It reaches for it.

B.AEAB) Story does not measure reality, nor is it measured by reality.

B.AEABA) Story is contained within fictive space, but seeks at each boundary to cross.

B.AEAC) A story makes a story.

B.AEAD) The relationships between the constituent parts of a story consist less in corresponding relations within a world than in negations of the relations and associations between storiemes within the fictive space.

B.AEAE) Where does the story touch reality?

B.AF) If a story is to represent a world, then it must sympathize with that world, build on its inherent relations and associations, then dismantle them.

B.AG) What a story must share with reality is the intersection where the accuracy of depiction loses currency and the fictive space opens as a swallowing abyss.

B.AGA) A story can tell any reality.

B.AGB) A story cannot represent itself, the form of itself, or its structure without sacrificing its form and so its reality.

B.AGC) A story may comment on its storyness to underscore or illustrate the *real* intersection, but fictive space collapses and disintegrates.

B.AGD) A story can exist outside itself, outside its structure, but not outside its form.

B.AHA) Every story has an internal logic and the breaking of a logic becomes a part of that logic. Therefore, within fictive space all is logical, provided the limits of the space remain intact.

B.B) A story presents a possible reality by creating the possibility of that reality within a fictive space.

B.B_A) Fictive space contains all the possibilities of a given story, its associations and relationships and the set-ordering of its constituent elements.

B.BA) A story is neither correct nor incorrect.

B.BB) A story is true.

B.BBA) A story represents itself.

B.BBB) A story may disagree with reality.

B.BBC) Reality may be false when regarded within a corresponding fictive space.

B.BBD) Reality has spatial and conceptual limitations.

C) Nothing is a story but a story.

Shades Are Just Dark Glosses

```
┌─────────────────┐    ═══    ┌─────────────────┐
│                 │    ═══    │                 │
│      sign       │           │      sign       │
│                 │           │                 │
└─────────────────┘           └─────────────────┘
```

RALPH

H

difference

What sits on the horizon for a far-sighted person is not the same for a near-sighted one. For the near-sighted, shipwrecked soul, there may be no rescue ship at all. But still when sighting of the vessel is reported, the near-sighted one does not complain by saying, "There is no ship on the horizon. It must be well beyond it." So, the plane passing through the center of the Earth and slicing space at the edge of vision, where Earth meets sky or water meets sky, is not relative, like something being a "stone's throw away," it being a matter of who might be throwing the stone. The horizon is where it is and when the presence of the *Beagle* is reported to a blind man, he knows the location of the ship. The horizon is never a stone's throw away, no matter how short-sighted one might be.

anfractuous

The fight was a messy and unsightly affair that spilled out from the chapel into the courtyard. Bloodied noses and lips curled in anger shown on every face. Mauricio moved his wife farther away, unable to pull her completely from the mission. Father Chacón was cranked with rage, though the emotion did not make him a better fighter. Each time he gained his feet, Jenny Jenson would deck him with a fist tethered to the round motion of her right arm. The cameraman was bleeding profusely from a gash on his forehead, but was managing to block the karate-style kicks of Father O'Blige. The soundman was pinned, face to the ground, beneath the girth of Father O'Boie. But no one saw me and so I scooted away through the irises and hid beneath a small lemon tree.

unties of simulacrum

Steimmel and Davis screeched to a stop on the street in front of the chapel.

pharmakon

Colonel Bill drove his Hummer over the low wall of the courtyard and slid to a murdering halt in the bed of irises.

ootheca

Mo parked on the street and walked through the main entrance of the mission. Barthes was some paces behind her.

tubes 1 ... 6

Steimmel, Davis, Colonel Bill, and Ferdinand joined in the fighting. Ferdinand knocked O'Boie from the soundman and sat on the man himself. Colonel Bill knocked Jenny Jenson silly with a punch. Steimmel knocked Colonel Bill down with a kick to the face. Davis stood in the middle of the action and looked around for me.

incision

habit
hiragana
hyperbole
heritor
hinge

umstände

My mere claim to existence, as a baby so *gifted,* must exist in the margins of sense, perhaps even as a vague shape or form on the horizon of logic, but if I lay claim to a kind of existential affirmative statement, *i.e., there is at least one baby who can write a paragraph,* am I running the risk of being perceived as a radical who denies the possibility of universals? Or am I picnicking with the likes of Tweedledee and Tweedledum? What are a nickel and four pennies?

subjective-collective

My mother approached the commotion, her eyes darting all around for me. Steimmel recognizing her, took a wild swing at Eve's face. Eve ducked and the blow connected solidly with Barthes' chin. Barthes stumbled forward, unconscious on his feet and fell against Davis, knocking her to the ground. My mother was on her knees and from there she spotted me under the lemon tree. She crawled quickly over to me and hugged me.

The reunion, even in the middle of the melee, was sweet and deeply felt. She stroked my head and I clung to her like, well, a baby. A gesture that I could tell she appreciated. She was weeping and, though I too was moved by the moment, I wanted her to get me out of there. I stiffened as a signal and she responded.

She covered me with her body and made her way to the section of low wall that Colonel Bill's Hummer had wrecked. She got me to the street and into her car and away we drove.

vita nova

My mother and I are living peacefully and secretly in a small coastal town. She now goes by the name Alice and she calls me Isadore. And so I guess I am Isadore. I am four now and I have little friends who belong to women who are more or less like Mo. They are stupid children, but I do not hold it against them. I have agreed with my mother that we should keep *me* a secret. So, at night we read and I write notes and she tells me what she thinks. My father does not know where we are. We know he didn't get the job at Texas and we know that he didn't get tenure and we know that Roland Barthes never read his article on alterity. But that's all we know. The Saab is long gone. My mother drives a Dodge Dart. She changed completely her way of painting and even she says now that the work is no good. She works at a drugstore. I love my mother and she loves me.

Vexierbild

In spite of my reunion with my mother, I learned that nothing comes full circle, but stretches out like a line, extending infinitely toward some ideal terminal point that is necessarily only a point, just like I am only a point on the line. But am I insignificant? No. The point is whole, the point is complete, but the line . . . the line is everything.

The *line* is everything.

PERCIVAL EVERETT is Distinguished Professor of English at the University of Southern California and the author of more than thirty books, including *Dr. No*, *The Trees*, *Telephone*, *I Am Not Sidney Poitier*, and *Erasure*.

The text of *Glyph* is set in Adobe Garamond type. Book design by Donna Burch. Composition by BookMobile Design & Digital Publisher Services, Minneapolis, Minnesota. Manufactured by Versa Press on acid-free 30 percent postconsumer wastepaper.